tell
tale
signs

Tell Tale Signs

fictions

Janice Williamson

Turnstone Press

Turnstone Press

607-100 Arthur Street
Winnipeg, Manitoba
Canada R3B 1H3

Turnstone Press gratefully acknowledges the assistance of the Canada Council and
the Manitoba Arts Council in the publication of this book.

Cover design: Marna Bunnell, Penumbra Associates.

Text design: Robert MacDonald, MediaClones Inc.
Toronto Ontario, Banff Alberta and Vancouver British Columbia

Author photo: Sima Khorrami.

This book was printed and bound in Canada by Kromar Printing Limited for Turnstone Press.

Canadian Cataloguing in Publication Data
Williamson, Janice
Tell tale signs
ISBN 0-88801-159-8
I. Title.
PS8595.I565T45 1991   C818/.54   C91-097159-5
PR9199.3.W556T45 1991

(a dedication)

an identical prairie low-flying blue scattered everywhere and cloudless a half century before her breaking stroke my grandmother's buggy gathers speed wraps body against the startling chill this spinster thirtyish turns toward a schoolhouse a lonely elevator with some relief from her orphaned childhood of domestic servitude (motherless at birth) of servile gratitude to foster home of pubescent amnesia at the death of her sister at fifteen in childbirth her sister now nameless — *did she ever know the love of a christian name?* impregnated in her room walls not even paper thin blankets between her and the hired hand or some animal come ripping into the loft to tear through walls wool nightie thin membranes of my grandmother's mind when she remembers to tell me this story at ninety-four white hair brilliant claims not to remember the rest of her childhood "did i do housework to put myself through normal school the only thing i knew how to do?" my grandmother asks as though between that midnight violation and the turn toward the schoolhouse burning in bitter cold my grandmother's body stretches taut in forgetting

The story reveals the meaning of what otherwise would remain an unbearable sequence of sheer happenings.

Hannah Arendt

Reality is what we recapture by an incalculable return of imaged things, like a familiar sense. . . . There must be, we think, another sense, another version since we dream of it as we do of a musical accompaniment, a centered voice capable of securing for us a passage, a little opening. A voice which could, at equal distance from origins and death, activate the hypotheses, adapt the adornment, adjust the folds, . . . regulate the alternating movement of fiction and truth.

Nicole Brossard
trans. Susanne de Lotbinière-Harwood

If you know the story, it's clearly visible.
If you don't know the territory, it's out of sight.

Mary Scott

Contents

tell
tale
signs

You were so generous, they told me,
allowing everything in its place,
but what we wanted to hear was a story.
Lyn Hejinian

There are signs our speech is in circulation. Yet we write within, alongside, a market with occasional exchange. She begins to address her audience, "Are you listening?" Some reply derisively, others with glee. Her talk is a restoration with a twist. Nervous laughter makes translation difficult. Useful clichés are introduced. There is some talk of "difference from," about "oppression" or the "difference within." Issues about the marginal are juxtaposed with exclusive cliques of the privileged. Her voice trembles at the gap.

Stories begin to speak themselves. From Nellie McClung's "let them howl" to "Mother" Willie Mae Ford Smith's enchanted songs and Emma's wordless tongue. Listeners begin with laboured breath to speak.

Nothing will be gained by finishing our tales.

We will not "get it right."

"how many smiles?")

The prostitutes compare notes with the receptionists. How many upturned eyes? How many disinterested gestures of interest? Did you hear the one about the ad agency? Copy-writers test their best ideas on their expert secretaries. The girl at the front desk gets the biggest unofficial praise. In her ante-room, the elevator door opens and closes every four and one-half minutes while she reads non-stop except when answering the telephone at three-minute intervals. Sometimes models make an appearance through this mechanical hole in the wall which slides soundlessly open. Framed in the cavernous vertical slit, the women rearrange their bodies; their minds anticipate vacant stares. Occasionally, on cloudless days, one will wear her see-through plastic raincoat which reveals nothing but luminescent breasts and palest skin. Outlining the contours of her liberation, this costume helps her get a job.

Fig. 3

In the first-page news photo, the eight strongest men in the world, ordered in a row of muscular arms, tug at the end of a rope. In the distance, an airplane appears to move in slow motion, or perhaps a missile flies ominously at night. White flashes of sweat appear on their bodies as they move without fuel like magic down the runway.

On the next page, two men and a woman are framed in an image of disaster. The men in fresh white coats face each other; their arms reach out to pull at the woman, naked and covered in mud. Autochthonic, she is borne in terror.

the reader's scent)

Apples and cheese in a city perfumed between jasmine and frangipani. Others chew on dried biscuits delivered for breakfast and lunch. After dinner the atmosphere shifts from cocktails to machine-gun fire in the suburbs. The picture isn't pretty, though the white sand beach remains. A tender ocean awaits.

Inland, the young white woman travels alone, mistaken for doctor or princess, unskilled but not disinterested. Old men are brought to her, their eyes filled with dry wind, with blindness. Young girls and boys hide bloody wounds beneath their skirts, hide behind their mothers. The stranger bathes their wounds, dispenses gauze and goodwill. At dusk, the wife of the nomadic chief invites her to ride a cherished white stallion through the tented camp. She canters with a degree of grace. Her dress billows with the desert breeze, then whips about her flowing hair. A spectacle of pale nakedness.

Dismounting, she is greeted by dignified applause. Onlookers present her with a zigzag silver ring; a tasselled amulet secreting a scrap of the Koran; a one-eyed monkey; a lively duck; a wicker pannier of dried meat; a tapestry of pictographs; a meal of rice and rancid butter; a carved wooden spoon. A white horse.

Fig. 5

Onlookers watch and listen while a bright mural freezes the movement of the women mid-sentence. Their hair is tied round in ornate fabric; their fists rise towards the upper left-hand corner of the image where clear sky surrounds them.

tried to find out what one meant exactly in life by the words bliss, passion, ecstasy, that had seemed to her so beautiful in books." These explorations led her through and along empty pre-dawn rooms, acrid corridors, rain-drenched paths. Rooting through catalogues and libraries, she searched for clues to her dilemma. New friends dimmed lights, taking her in turn to dance until all hollows disappeared.

Emma's head tilts toward a frame of drapery. The wheels of a cart's progress trundle in darkness. Her maid has lit candles, laid out silky petticoats on plump feather pillows. In the bath Emma tells her stories, peopled with tender fingers and slippery beasts. Between chapters, her music swells, a repetitive suture of movement. She imagines the probing glass rods, the submarine flesh folded into itself. She can smell the taste; her sounds muted and caught.

Fig. 8

The gnawing inside her body is thought by others to be imagined. After a while she grows accustomed to pain's contours; the rhythms arch her back eloquently when watched. No other symptoms appear in spite of the camera. Experts say again and again there is nothing to treat, nothing to which she might surrender. Echoes inside her chest are without significance; measured responses, unremarkable.

Fatigue plagues her. When the lumps appear, the same experts change their tune; they were "anticipated." To monitor what ails her, a sequence of three tests is devised and named: "Emily 1," "Emily 2" and "Western Block." The results are positive. Her whole body is wrapped in plastic, then photographed. Her skin shines brilliant throughout; even the spaces between her fingers cast shadows. The treatment takes place in a silent retreat. At first the prognosis is good, though progress slow. Later, contemplation and writing infect her. She suffers a relapse.

the narrator sorts herself out)

It was particularly the case after she read the newspaper report of how he had "become interested in survivalism, tribulation theology and the theory of hard economics." He had his ideas; she had hers. She made no claims for resolution.

Even now, in sleep, puddles of water seep across the surface of her eyes. He would reach down towards her and muddy the water, as though it mattered whether they touched or she responded in kind. Occasionally she would press down on her eyelids. Night, until light began to dissolve on rain-soaked highways. Then she drifted to meet another woman, someone you might have recognized. As she stood impatiently, her hair was shorter than in memory, her skin a wash of metallic glitter. There were no photographs to document their touch.

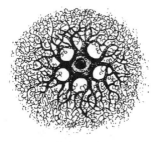

Fig. 11

When she sleeps on her left side, most of her organs press down, undifferentiated, one upon the next — like a story, "one thing following any other." Somewhere inside they said there was something the size of an orange, perhaps a grapefruit. As she turned, pain verified the location, though precise dimensions were uncertain. Sometimes she strained to overhear their conversation . . . *barren . . . childless.* . . . Or she would imagine how a tropical pebbled surface might rupture, flesh split open and dripping. How it felt. Inside out.

the author makes a play for the reader)

He contemplates the relation between women and fish with a passion. Blood is drawn like water to the bath where her frenzied kicks contact the cruel brass of rushing faucet. It is a joke. She nods, gasping for air. Listen to her breath, the sounds of her own laughter.

It's possible the woman who remembers this now is a different woman. No one remembers her then, when she disappeared south of the border to find true happiness where it must have gone. Somewhere between two places, between Canadian Tire and Loblaws for example, or variations on this theme.

One of these public spaces fills up with people who cook Continental dishes with some ease. Others come to prepare their refried beans, to shuffle in bedroom slippers through tiers of tinned goods. She is white; they are not. The bars fill with good music. She never enters. At home, he never listens. She cooks and cooks and cooks and then she kicks open his head with the back of her heel. His brains break loose. Lizards across the parquet. The photographs do not capture. The heat. Rust-filled breaths escape this written account.

Fig. 14

"I write down a fiction of your arm." A hair-line fracture, broken in jest. You cry out, extend your wrist towards me. Tenderly I grasp the trembling limb and watch fine bones shift and return to their places. Only this difference remains: the edges in shadow invisible to the eye.

the reader takes a second look)

The doorbell rings at midnight. An unidentified neighbour announces, "My mother is sick. Will you tend the babies for half an hour?"

Sick mothers are hard to refuse. You agree, and then you're there in the midst of babies and boxes and the stench of their confluence. Waiting. You watch an aging TV talk-show host interview a former talk-show host interview a starlet whose show has been cancelled. In the light of this electronic long poem of failure, the living room brightens. What if this unnamed woman refuses to return? What if the three darling children, unclaimed, were to float into your living room for twenty years and whisper madonna visions dedicated to this lost night?

You needn't have worried. Forty minutes later, right on time, the woman returns with a tall tale, an outlandish itinerary of accidents and missed streetcars. In the middle of her story a cab driver, identified only as her former boyfriend, appears like a clue. Just as the listener had anticipated, she refused his ride. Just as she would refuse interrogation, were it necessary. But the trick is caught in the tag of her dress, reversed, and now visible. Somewhere, there was a quick blow job. A hot flush, and then she is gone. Out of the car, into the cab, or along the snow-filled sidewalk to where a stranger kept watch over her household.

The two women say goodnight. She introduces herself as "Diane."

Fig. 17

The silver bowl fills with water, a swish swish swimming sound with a clatter. Just before the shattering of glass, a mistake, rubber gloves squeal along the surface. Boxes and boxes of boxes and inside the diapers fold neatly one on top of the other. One reaches in to find another and then the baby cries, impatient. The hand retreats.

the reader responds in kind)

She knew her right from her left, though they claimed a middle way would accomplish everything. Over time, this had not proven true. The players changed but many replicated their actions through generations. Hanging on for signs to alert them to change, they misread heroines and villains, collaborators and conspirators. Occasionally simulated transvestites, despite superficial goodwill, manifested a familiar reflex, resentment.

Alternatives surfaced. But all his disembodied body talk (not the strain that breeds muscles) bored her to death. Infected by the dialectic of desire, of difference, of displacement, she attributed his paragraphs to a smart blazon at the entrance to privileged Hollywood property.

At night, her skin crawled. She wanted to sit and sit and sit, to waste away, like Echo, letting her bones speak. As tradition would have it, there would be no response.

Fig. 20

A famous gossip pushes aside her files of bona fide interviews and leans towards the reporter. Yes, she replies, I am famous. Yes, she replies, I write exclusively about those more famous than myself. Yes, she replies, I write about those I loathe. Yes, she replies, I am powerful. Yes, she replies, I know what is happening and what is not. Yes, she replies, I wield my power like a lion. Yes, she replies, I roar like a lamb.

tropics of conversation)

Gossips, "god-related" in medieval times, attend births in the company of nurses and midwives. "Horner in *The Country Wife* knows how sexual news circulates — through females and the powerless." In 1811 gossip announced the flippery of women's talk.

No longer the case, now rumorous gossip resounds with the loud confusion of verb-tubed bazookas. Christians called gossips murderers. In all this noise, who knows what here? Those in the know are intended to know; those in the dark are not players. An upstairs woman, the insomniac, writes memos, working to stem the tide of institutional talk. Criminal conversations circulate through halls, electric with bitter voltage.

Consider these gothic wounds: your subject of conversation, a tongueless spectre.

Fig. 26

Conversation rooms keep our voice company, honour our friendships. Sidney's *Arcadia* revealed in 1580 that "She went to Pamela's chamber, meaning to joy her thoughts with the sweet conversation of her sister." "Converse," so lately a word designed to talk, was earlier "the act of living or having one's being *in* a place or *among* persons." In contemporary Harlem, conversation signals Toni Cade Bambara's "touch talking." "In a place or among persons," our hearing's thin skin weeps stories. A textual tourniquet to stop the flow of malice.

dear reader)

A yoga devotee defines varieties of "bliss." "Number 8 — BEYOND BODY CONSCIOUSNESS," she says. "Or, Number 7? Perhaps this might suit you — EMBODIED BLISS."

Between two mental landscapes, the sea returns a face she dreams and loves; one who argues there are no sceptics in paradise. Between the dream of violence, of loss, "the other side of fear," and this figuration of pleasure, warmth, comfort and acknowledgement, a painful skin is shed on the beach. In the long hiatus inside noon, her heart's chronometer shifts undertone; suspended waves of voice clock a different rhythm. On the cliff, attentive tourists establish their version of narrative distance. Glimpse a naked thigh, a hand thrust under the towel. His head disappears — or is it her? Lost. Her head so slow to turn; eyes, a pale moon, the verb of moan. From above, we re-enact our own stories, raptures between this place and there. The view was where we found it. The distance between two figures wrapped in sand and those windblown and watching speaks your own kind of want.

Fig. 27

Euphoria skinned alive. A last ocean wave fills the screen. Lips, eyes, lines along a forehead. His white edge breaks across her arms. She dreams the usual: a shooting — a man with a brass arm, the sinister one, and another woman, armed to the hilt. An urgent nurse moves towards their disappearance. Twin blasts tear at their bodies; blistered surfaces expand in thick air. Raw and mute, the man-woman battle as one. Fears end downstairs in the factory where she imagines herself baled upwards by machine. Bailed out? Or an assembly line re-entry; the only way to fly.

the writer reads her title page)

The signature is illegible. Not smudged or faded by turning pages and the years, but incomprehensible in original figuration: a script with no shared readings: an orthography based on absence. The imaginary language traces the gaps, the spaces between. The interrupted line across the page, a face of snow tracked in the wilds. First it appears to mean one thing, then another. A controversy erupts. Hieroglyphs come to light.

Picture this. The book is unearthed in the future. Passed from hand to hand by a panel of experts (mutilated in form), decoded time after time in open forums and proclamations. How-to hypotheses keep the public awake to history. Authorities speculate and pronounce. Critics rally round to insist original authorship is close at hand. Was the signature rooted in the Indo-European? Was it a male or female hand? Is it a technical manual or the practice of the avant-garde? Is the rumour of translation true? Does it really say, "Madam, I'm Adam"? "Frankly, I don't give a damn"? Or is it more literally abecedarian?

Fig. 31

This solitude is not an I hook. The letters are returned to a sender, not quite I. This strange loop Eli might have noticed right off. But I plead ignorance and let loose my fingertips' measured rhythms . . . .

Whenever I gets into the picture, you always hovers around the frame. Some remain unconvinced of your presence, though I, having remained so long in your shoes, can verify everything. At least for the moment.

You noted in the early part of the century, "The pool opened onto an empty room." It could have been an isolated tale of the always already spoken, of defeat. The borders could have been described as a barren landscape, but you preferred a looser interpretation. All this in your writing: an unprecedented subtlety of movement, the shifting light, your lushness pressing out towards me.

dear "Ruined Appetite")

You charge that reviewer Janet Free's use of language is "inappropriate, offensive and ultimately unimaginative" in describing a certain pie at Thumper's restaurant as "orgasmic." Your point is well taken. We appreciate that if eating a pie is Ms. Free's method of obtaining sexual gratification, you "certainly don't wish to be informed." However we're certain Ms. Free meant the word in a colloquial sense, not as literal definition. In the future, we will try to avoid such misunderstandings.

Fig. 33

Sweat beads her brow, knitted in concentration, labouring ecstatically towards gratification. Orgasm: the colloquial kind assisted by new technology. A Braun electric toothbrush slithers pulsating across her lips. Clear plastic bristles knot in twisted tendrils. The impenetrable underbrush, the jumbled contours of her dark continent undulate. The room hums with desire, Duracell, and her everyday articulations. This conversation, a sound poem of *jouissance*, extends, apparently, forever. A perverse thought of coconut creme interrupts her body's quickened rhythms. Shortening's greased touch stiffens her nipples above flaky crusts rolled round her belly. A storm of white on white, blinding, sifts through her consciousness. Sticky limbs slide along the hot assembly line of baked goods. Transparent gloves handle her roughly. Pinch, then test, her every surface . . .

She drifts deep into waves of milky secretions, floats in desire's cream-filled heart. Whipped, she surfaces whole in symphonic crescendo.

the narrator travels abroad)

At breakfast in Brussels the blonde apologizes before her piano, tunes up with scales, coffee trembling. The fanfare orchestrated in three weeks for a small symphony blasts along the street, lifts up sparkling veils of Moroccan market women. Silver threads unravel and catch wind through Horta's art nouveau swirls. Doilies string along laced-up city fountains. Sift through postcards in the square to find a little boy with big prick who pees everywhere exported to America. Hitler eyed the sphinx-columned grandeur of the National Palace a mall long; the story goes, he cherished it enough to ensure that only rare buildings were bombed out during the war. In peace time, glass gilt halls flow raspberry beer. Bring on the splendid feather-bearing dancing girls in the Latin Bar. All in one car the rich men and women cruise the fluorescent blue lane of the red-light district where leather-jacketed women cops with matte-black handbag-sized machine guns stand guard. Two hold up tequila for good. Black champagne *girls* from the Belgian Congo tell you straight out how much they hate their job. When no one listens, the banker talks culture and jogging. (Behind the dance floor in the back room a skinny man gets a fast blow job.) At the bar, a white woman debates feminist ethics with an emphatic Swiss man; later, sweating, she dances with the women.

Fig. 36

Your body, he writes, makes the rest of the world less hostile.

the reader trips out)

In Amsterdam, step gables order our reflection. Drunk with jet lag she insists gables are bagels; her garbled listening is intent inside smoke-filled bars. Daytime rambling tourists plod the sixty-minute route through galleries, finding masterpieces wherever they look. Along the canal, souvenirs exchange money. The ballerina woman drifts closer; her tulle skirt stiffens above net stockings slashed in a crisscross puzzle of razorblades. This a sign for your attentive whispers to search below.

"In the summer streets of Amsterdam, loving tattoos have been slit and punctuated by her cigarette's livid end," one woman wrote the next morning in her hotel-room journal. The other woman, sleepless and "negative," remembers reading the French feminist novel set in the *duende* land of lithesome death. The heroine falls into deep silence on hearing the Spanish dance. Her hand, suspended motionless above the table, becomes a spectacle of the same fiery pain. With the hiss of quick inhalation, the others (her lover [a woman], her lover's lover [a man], and the writer) gasp the stench. Her palm opens to the glow of a blistered heart.

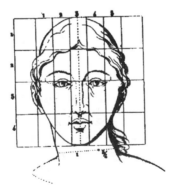

Fig. 37

A high yellow note is our morning greeting. In Amsterdam, step gables order our reflection. A tenor saxophone blasts across gallery walls cracked in a crisis of regard. Across the corridor, black and white studies of gnarled hands move in flight across the canvas. You compare them to the trees your German father drew on the Russian front. Do they twist into the silent weapon your solitude assumes?

At the theatre, a Chinese poet rubs his leg in pain and says the rest of the world is no less hostile. She writes him *high yellow notes throat songs to winter want high wanting yellow this note a counterpoint to pain*

"lonely begonia,")

the now deceased sound poet intoned in 1971. In her early twenties, she couldn't write with capital letters because bpNichol had been irresistible with his unforgettable memory and a smile which sent her beyond eros to language's smooth ledge. On National Arts Centre floor cushions, all cultural attachés and diplomats listened to the poet's song. This was permitted before the current rule of fake chandeliers.

She thought bp's "lonely begonia" poem was an adult joke until twenty years later she read: "Solitude on the level of the world is a wound we do not need to comment on here." Concluding that Blanchot had not heard of angel-wing begonias, she pursued this subject in the light of once pink blossoms scattered across her desk like so many orbit fictions knit together in Carl's basement where Jamaican drums and Ottawa Valley beer flowed with the original Taj Mahal. Good days followed with bread knives and fruitcake drugs cut hot; hallucinations were more fabled than death.

(All this returns when she makes love to the black jazz vinyl, spun round and round, when she catches sight of that first woman, a shiver of feigned indifference caught in a curl of hair.

Fig. 41

Now that the '90s had been broached, she could speak about how her '60s began in 1969 with a great rustle of attention to optimistic new initiatives and our legacy of human cruelty. We took this in stride as though laughter would drown out the status quo. We thought we could grow old together knowing justice and, as a result, in retrospect, many blamed others for failure. We were surprised thirty years later on hearing an older woman at dinner announce defensively, "I love to cook," as though she cited a pleasure beyond our imagining. We feared the stuttering double-barrelled vowels of birth announcements were the only site of social transformation. Mass rallies defended kitchen rights while battered women fled their homes. Heterosexuality appeared to be on the upswing, especially in the ruling residential regions where boredom may be more widely received.

the narrator encounters comparative despair)

How could she tell him her reading of Marguerite Duras was ruptured and superimposed on nothing but memory? Her own. She was writing (as in critic) a paragraph about how there was no space left in the melancholic blankness of her prose to embroider anything but a cool impassive voyeuristic look of the Duras reader she imagined. "The reading of the book will act as theatre for the story." Too close for comfort, she reads on: "One night, she asks him if he could do it with his hand, but without coming close to her, without even looking. He says he couldn't. . . ." She finishes the book, masturbates. Turning to another novel, *The War*, she recognizes her own photograph taped to the wall of the '40s Paris apartment. She calls into this sentence: "I need room again to suffer." Was it vulgar opportunism which allowed her to recuperate "to suffer" at this place, this reading, this time of no war, of no lost lover? And yet, she could see through the mask of Duras' face; lines of alcoholic tears ring her mouth.

Fig. 42

She reads.
    The book ends — "They are happy as they've ever been before. A happiness so profound it frightens them . . . surging through the words."
    The dog howls.
    The poet writes her heart, wet melodrama of leached sinew. This hollow familiar story.

the plot recalls)

Only these fractured words are called to mind. She pinpoints her anguish at the moment her father . . . But this is where the voice becomes confused. According to her, he played the piano, was limited, narrow, unimaginative and unwise. According to her older woman writer friend, his black turtleneck, lithe samba, slow jazz blues made him romantic. She confesses she once upon a time had a fever: her father took her temperature while mother was in the kitchen. Later he killed himself. No connection mattered other than the knotted whip of his limbs. This aquamarine accident didn't really happen; his heart filled with thick floating disease, a jewelled coral head.

His daughter would be lost without him (her tutu tight pubescent body sways to his tinkling ivories; his slow smile breaks fortissimo). She would marry a neo-fascist (thigh muscles knot at night to gruesome cries), drop out of school, take up decorating, home renovating, deep gourmet cooking. She would do her job swell (silk shantung hot pink slit to inside seams tucked double), obsessively (stitch welt pockets cowl neck cover up), with no concern for the future (she knows, trapped:

Fig. 45

. . . she has no memory of this. She's making it up. It never happened. She doesn't remember. She'll get him into trouble. It wasn't him. It was the other one. She's lying. She's doing it for her own good. She'll get it in the end. She's not to be trusted. It's her creative imagination. She's unreliable. It's a conspiracy. There'll be trouble to pay. . . . (Afternoons she weeps with soap opera heroines: murderous daughters, polished blonde mothers. All women turn to look at the camera a split second too long before credits roll quickly and viewers miss their names.)

In the office, the student and the teacher face off to talk about their work, the stress of too many classes, his new therapeutic chairs. She looks at the view behind his back where an eagle's flight astonishes a big prairie sky. Bodies slide under words clothed in thought. Flesh tones touch the attentive reader. He considers her thighs, breasts, throat — their soft turn under his hand. Talking together, she recognizes his longing, feels something similar, though muted.

The man and woman wait inside each other's syllables. She refuses him silently on the grounds that to let her body lie in his workplace is to give up her mind; he denies his desire, fearful of her hesitation, or worse, her caress. When they make love, he audibly names her anatomical parts.

If you were to stand facing the toilet bowl, you could read this dusty note propped on top of his white porcelain tank: "Babel feared he would become an intellectual, a man *with spectacles on his nose and autumn in his heart.*"

Fig. 46

Pick the story up and throw it across the street into someone else's living room; walls light up with the bright being of a Pentecostal thrilled with her dream. Inventing the bomb which fell just outside the window, she embellishes and calls the others in chapel to clear out, run for cover. Some lag behind. Unbelievers are abandoned as she runs towards the hills.

(Why doesn't she like this novel?)

she says, "I'm thinking through my body")

He says, "There's music at the heart of thinking." In the restaurant, they have a conversation. She sips tawny port and waits for the pain in her ovaries to subside.

"What's eating you?"

Nothing. Hysterical symptoms or displaced anxiety about performing as intellect not body, she thinks, as though the two were not entangled. A "daydreamer," she is distant, elsewhere.

At the table, above the snapper, consciousnesses float like dessert. As the philosophers talk, she wonders how her writing can ever replicate the starburst gold pin flecked with diamonds suspended on a crisp black linen sheath directly across the damask-white table. The conversation shifts to department politics and the impending suicide of colleagues. Gloomy, they speak with hushed concern about desperation, abandonment, fierce loneliness or madness. What is to be done?

Over and over, she tells how her student had stretched out on her husband's apartment carpet, taken pills, cut her wrists, and lived to compose the poem "Sylvia Sylvia" with arterial ease. There is a comparison of scars. Repetition hides the cries.

Fig. 51

I am sitting here. I want to locate myself inside this conversation, a little drunk, heady with talk. Our bodies fill up and empty words. State your preference about the erotics of listening, an exchange which moves through beyond outside inside these synaptic gaps. Singing in tongues transports, hits the limit of aphorisms. Rally round. Sing willy nilly about the ways the monologue holds your head.

dog M investigates author/reader contract)

Older, lethargic, he lifts his tired eyes towards her, anticipating food, play (a scratch), affection. She imagines she has two lovers: one male, one female. The woman, a few years younger, can't stop touching her, her longing is always in the air. After lunch and talk, their walks always lead towards a bed where they curl up in mirrors, stroke reflections. In the soft hollow above the collar-bone, they catch tears, talk about love, how they wish, how they can't. They talk about their mothers: one abandoned, the other enmeshed in thin-skinned confusion. One loves too much; the other too little.

Later she looks at her lover through his eyes the colour of sandfilled shallows, his eyes fill with water mammal knowledge somewhere between sympathy and cold comfort, beast of some turquoise deep. She imagines his amphibious thoughts under the surface. They watch a bad movie, hold hands, sweating, almost to the end.

In order to preserve their time together, apart, they maintain discipline and leave separately. He is thoughtful and only speaks unpunctuated phrases for emphasis. At the moment, he insists on her modest intelligence. Solitudinous desire narrows the corridor between want and denial. His body says goodnight. He walks her to her car. Her step quickens with disappointment, rage: a wrist-flung book catches on the red velour car seat. Pages fold back to this:

. . . the car door slams . . .

Fig. 53

The car door slams.
She doesn't look back.
There is fury.
Sorrow.
Reconciliation.

the readers wax lunar)

How they love, they do, each other. How she wants more of him than he will give (an old story). He holds on to this ungiving, controls his every gesture, kisses only when kissing is likely to lead nowhere. Or when the time is right. He fears her desire, or does his want trip him up? She holds on to her longing, hoping it won't seep out, humiliated into a tantrum, or astonish her mid-conversation. She writes libido into her daybook. Beside appointments with dentist, therapist, students, desire looks like a deadline. Pen mid-air, she tries to imagine whether this day or that will be libidinally favourable. What will he be thinking? Writing? Or more to the point, what will she be thinking? Is this a factor since she is paralysed with longing? Unable to write. To think. This has nothing to do with him. The block, the crick in her neck between head and hand; the silence began a while ago. Was it libido or listening?

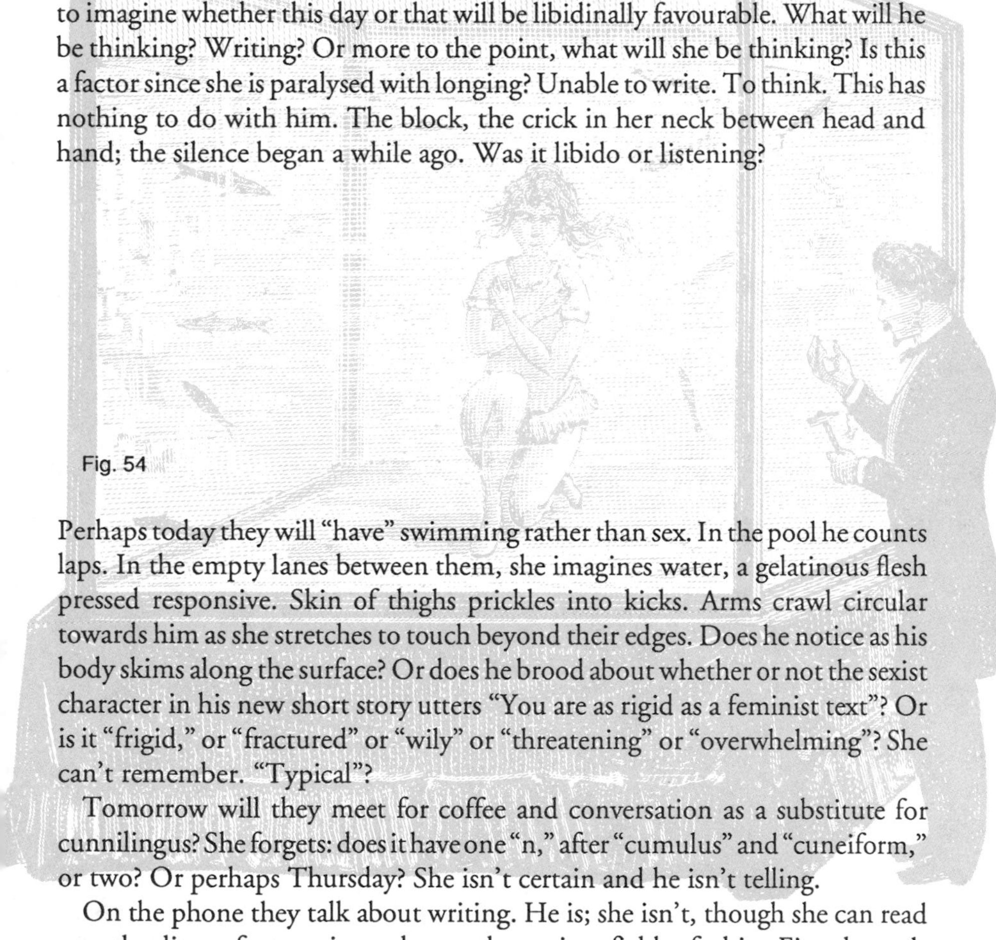

Fig. 54

Perhaps today they will "have" swimming rather than sex. In the pool he counts laps. In the empty lanes between them, she imagines water, a gelatinous flesh pressed responsive. Skin of thighs prickles into kicks. Arms crawl circular towards him as she stretches to touch beyond their edges. Does he notice as his body skims along the surface? Or does he brood about whether or not the sexist character in his new short story utters "You are as rigid as a feminist text"? Or is it "frigid," or "fractured" or "wily" or "threatening" or "overwhelming"? She can't remember. "Typical"?

Tomorrow will they meet for coffee and conversation as a substitute for cunnilingus? She forgets: does it have one "n," after "cumulus" and "cuneiform," or two? Or perhaps Thursday? She isn't certain and he isn't telling.

On the phone they talk about writing. He is; she isn't, though she can read now that lines of typescript no longer shatter into fields of white. First the curls and slivers of ink form hieroglyphs, meaning too approximate for display. Now the letters add up to words but she no longer knows where she fits into the picture. What is HER reading? How DOES she produce without desire? It isn't his fault.

the figure navigates her route)

Nothing is fixed: everything, except tornadoes, anticipated — drought, blizzard, mid-winter mid-afternoon dusk. Psyches and seasons appear as inevitable and manic-depressive as the moon. In summer, sunsets near midnight and unbroken cloudless skies torment farmers, thrill city dwellers and West Coast expatriates. The lens, radiant, rests a moment too long on the tempered bliss of these upturned faces: where there is smoke there are fires leaping thick and deep across eight thousand hectares east of Rocky Mountain House. Smell the back-burned air. Last month the morning newspaper featured another fire different only in kind: twenty-seven people trapped on the freeway by the windswept smoke of a farmer's strategically set fire. A culture/nature conundrum: what's good for the crops kills commuters. Indeed, there were paint-peeling burns, smoke inhalation, sudden deaths. Tired city workers returning south to Millet lost direction in a shadow blizzard, a photographic landscape ruined in brilliant flash. Drifting in this fogged skinless space, lungs light up with heaving smoke. Each driver carefully accelerates into the trunk of the car in front. Navigating their deaths, the passengers — husbands, neighbours, wives and lovers — press to their bodies the thin mapped line of the Trail, red to Red Deer. Slivered metal membranes cut the heat, their horror, the barren land.

Fig. 58

On the Drop of Doom there is so much to say and only six seconds to feel the separation. The interior of the body drops out of the body (not exactly): the resurrection of the organs is driven home (read head). Teenage boys tell you where, how to look. Down. Eyes focus between our legs line up metal grid perpendicular with steel track now tracking. Down. Three seconds and the body rises out of itself. Skinned. Alive. Reminds us — our thinking — how we locate ourselves above.

lost tale spins)

Face posed, fixed up by the door. Like all but a few of the others she worked to enclose herself in the familiar. Our everyday echo chamber resounded: ASTON-ISHING LONGING, LOST HOPE, INCREDIBLE NOSTALGIA.

But this chorus, a history of connection, is not central to the story. Transplanted west, she reads *Peterina to the Rescue*. Unapologetic about her misery, she ignores all calls to courage: mountain climbing, homesteading, calf-breaking, jelly making, cowcatcher-riding frontierswomen possess something she does not. Prairie women stand up. Frozen to sculpted stoicism season after season, mahogany-branched dogwood cast brave shadows across white, grow leaf thick in spring. Uprooted and planted into this prairie garden, she imagines herself clematis — a high yellow note clings to the back fence. Narcissistic gold fades to autumn wisps of fruit, fragile to darkness. Root-threatened bone-numb winter kill.

Fig. 60

Quicksilver, a fish, her mind darts here and there sucking at roots, pulling out tender white dream stems. From nightmares of loss and abandonment, stories tell too much of what she knows and doesn't know: stories about herself, by herself.

a migrant reader anticipates the familiar)

NOW is now and she has no television. Unknown to her, different soap opera women perform variations of the familiar under the same name. He, her husband, his children, his computers, his new brunette wife (the same name, can you believe it?) have moved back to Europe, bankrupt. She now lives in a more modest house, more remote city, divides her life into two overlapping categories of public/private: work/play. She can't stop writing endlessly about her work, her job, her desires, her body. Doubts surface: "Will I forever suffer the slur of mustard rape-seed across my being?" Haunted by the memory of Manitoba summers, she averts the eager colonial gaze southward from Toronto to New York.

A concerned colleague asks if she is undergoing a "make-over," in quotations, as though she is contagious. She considers trimming her bushy eyebrows, etc. Gazing dully across the parade of backyard garages, she contemplates removing herself to an imposing riverbank, a Wayne Gretzky twelfth or twentieth floor. Acres of bungalow lights twinkle towards the horizon, then switch off where the silent nothing of taiga begins.

Fig. 61

BIG as the big JESUS splashed across the side of the Calgary Trail grain elevator, the moon glides upward, diminishing in diameter as it arcs across the city. She thinks of her body, of food, of fuel — of the future of her body and what's left of her mind. Always there is something she ought to be doing, something other than what she is doing, something she should have been doing, impeccably, already.

the writer explores the Great North)

Slip step, chassé round the room, zoom long look through snow ravine. Camera lens dog-like in debris, suburban detritus. Hair now wind-swept, touch of gel smoothed to fuzz soft-focus edge. Cruise long look past war canoes. Paddling backwards, Paul Kane drifts the long river sometime after Native women occasioned his words. Sometime after The Famous Canadian Writers in search of The Famous Canadian Explorers wrapped themselves in how many yards of The Famous Canadian Netting and set out on foot, The Famous Canadian Players in The Famous Canadian North where The Famous Canadian Native Painters set up shop and missiles dive through spirit lines in among The Famous Canadian Location of Lac La Biche inhabited by The Famous Canadian Mothers (and largest Muslim population per capita) who flow through The Famous Canadian Peace River, never known to have inspired same. Long look through wolf willow, aspen clack clack poplar whittle-song in the air.

Fig. 63

Shrovel shrovel, my bleary mud-coated look gets into the car, something about naked ladies on the radio all the way to West Edmonton Mall. . . . Drive drive, she said, all the time his wet nose pressed to the window. Neighbourhoods streak stucco livid with green under glass.

the writer shops till she flops)

His kinetic sculpture is at the opposite end of the Mall. She calls it (how thoughtless) the "banal" region. No canals. No Hollywood pyrotechnics. No simulations of elsewhere: be here now at this water's edge at this large (larger) moment of history. "Discover new continents of pleasure," a perfumed Christopher Columbus intones beneath his gilt-edged Santa Maria, her polyethylene simulations of beached timber. On this chemical beach, large waves of pleasure await weekend guests: westward machines heave up surges of white-capped (reduced non-saline, six possible wave types all the way to surfing height) crests. None of this. No peacock tails strut under glass. No *croissants.* No *pain au chocolat.* No Europa Boulevard fake paintings duplicating every other fake painting everywhere else except China (you remind me) where fakery has its place in museums. In the east, the affront of duplication is diminished by skill: our pleasure is in laboured calligraphic strokes. Here, Medieval Dungeons invite tourists to "the dark side of history," rewarding courage with Michael Jackson tickets. Sell signs of torture beside glassed-in cases of crown jewels: real. (Take my word for it.)

Fig. 66

Later she thinks about the other side of her banal: the kinetic sculpture. Wooden blocks sound hard. Steel drum roll balls move circular reduce speed circumference drop through centre hole one by one, not quite slow until — watch — the final disappearance. A caught lift from and rising up forked metal fingers catch (just in time) rise up and drop, through space. Ball (wood) lingers. The length of an arc rail past a fat man, towards two one-eyed spider monkeys (once again, under glass) holding fingers to ears. Crash of cymbals. Time's up. More muzak. No lingering while under too much colour (with the you) a domed prairie blue sky dotted miniature yellow golf balls catch a ride towards a second floor named first. Our chartreuse lock-step balances heels' metallic click.

the writer takes note)

There are two things he notices in the Mall: the skaters' pleasure and the kinetic sculpture. Not the monument to socialist realist men, their monstrous bronze biceps drills through the centre of an Albertan earth. Bronze hands grip pipelines heading south: a toil larger than life. Inconspicuous dinosaurs list in shifting sands. He does not notice the handcuffed cussing New Orleans prostitutes in plaster; the pair of woman's legs emerging from an upper-storey window (her scream removed); the Mardi Gras travesties of the *Pays Dogon.* (This is not true. He mentions them in passing.) They do not notice in detail how the women behind the counter share gossip, oblivious to whether or not the fountains dance hourly to Beethoven's Ninth.

Fig. 67

This is not a seduction. She assures him this is the case. Though she cannot help the way she thinks through her body. Imagine this a compensation for the way her mind scurries along the marble floors, looks for clues, collects debris. . . . She thinks "marble" — the cool touch baffling sounds' babble only insofar as she and the woman across the Mall look up to hear each other speak loud now. Pop song: the way you walk.

the epistolary romances)

Upstairs and down, they write their letters about the serious side of desire, its relation to production. "How does one produce without desire?" Do they intend the question differently? Estelle flips through Woodward's Christmas catalogue looking for vibrating apparatus to assist her writing's progress. Last season, The Bay sold out their vibrators before she could reach the store. "A run on stiff necks?" she asked the clerk who smiled serenely, satisfied at her own bargain purchase.

At home, the other woman is certain of her desire, matching cheek to cheek the full pressure of breasts inside woollen February sweaters. Outside nothing is happening. The world "passes by." Events dissolve between backyards. Magpies litter the white lawn; blue jay brothers play at diversion from the main drift. "The world is passing by, beyond," she writes. Objects come into their own and begin to act only when we find ourselves familiar with their possibilities. But here there is a strangeness in the landscape: clipped sculpted shapes across the street, bushes green with waiting.

Fig. 70

At least this is how they appear to the two women writing, one up, one down: serious and because they remain so serious, they talk about ambivalence as a sign of maturity. Estelle considers how unsettling passion can become when met with certain knowledge.

the reader changes her tune)

Inside, shoppers gather on the hour for the musical interlude. Parked outside the cowboy hats and lace-up dance dresses, flames bust through the fountain to the tunes of the Neapolitan Alessandro Scarlatti. Fitting, she muses, since this place like the maestro's own "Singing City" Naples lies somewhere between Vesuvius and the sea. Her companion jots notes, mouthing his words while leaning on the large replica of a whale fitted out with a red velour thinking seat where a stalagmitic azygous uvula muscle might have protruded to beat about intruders' heads had it ever appeared in living whales to perform anything more than sonic whistles. Leaning against the large replica of the whale (dull bronze finish) he notes (the usual present tense and professorial tones) Scarlatti's "genius for writing eminently singable melodies wedded to clear tonally-centred harmony." Readers (Dear Reader) catch the languid lexicon, the language of romance. Pages turn more quickly: feverish talk about newly articulated corporeal folds and surfaces rub together, cross, uncross (probably silk taffeta in symmetrical executive maroon stripes). Catch the first notes of Scarlatti's *sinfonia*, prelude to the full-blown opera about to begin on ice. A break into song: three movements — quick, slow, quick — and it's like, fundamental, a little Neapolitan homophonic texture. Tiny metal holes in the ceiling send out sinfonic warnings. Their eyes light up passers-by. Blades are heard burring to sharpen. Bwaaaaaaaaaa . . . . . alarms sound. Veil self-control; cool confidence, quick wit. With joy. With joy jamming the works, dash the bronze unbronzed.

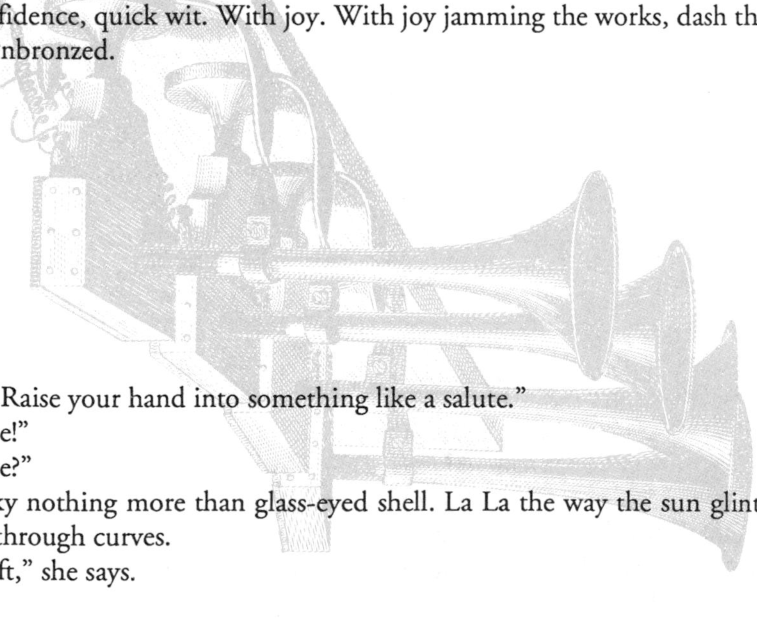

Fig. 72

"Estelle! Raise your hand into something like a salute."
"Estelle!"
"Estelle?"
The sky nothing more than glass-eyed shell. La La the way the sun glints straight through curves.
"So soft," she says.
"Yes."
So so

almost listening, the writer put down the phone)

Now that she has a job, she rarely answers the telephone. The gap between the all-encompassing arms of her imagination and the voice on her machine is so great she sometimes can't recognize the connection. Is this to her advantage? As she doodles small-loop shamrocks, four-leafed figures towards an undetermined future, she maintains the fiction of her past, the sense of completeness that wells up as she re-stages her life in the imagined warmth of so many others. She would have liked to stand by them in the midst of their sorrow, but she had been wounded by the limiting words of her own bourgeois class. Propriety and fear of nothing narrowed her life to a symptom of the full-blown.

Fig. 73

They didn't like her haircut or colour and, earlier that year, her habit had been to continue to eat simply. February she ate only cucumbers; then March and melons; April, avocados; May, marshmallows; June, jujubes (all but the black). She loved carrots but was wasting away in the hot August of artichokes, not knowing how to alphabetize her desire. In 1975, she wanted to move on to tomatoes.

she says that we're here, "north of intention")

At the market, the dollar's down. Afternoons, they steal each other's words. She "rips off" hers, is caught shoplifting; he commandeers his phrases with an air of authority, calls it "intertextuality." One of the poets won't, can't stop saying, "I am no feminist essentialist." We believe him.

After the market closes, well-appointed dance partners pair off: rhumba — Transcendence and the Quotidian; tango — street-wise Vulgar Feminist and Discrete Semiotician; non-stop tarantella — exotic Post-Russian Formalist and wild-eyed Discourse Analyst. During the last set, Ideology dismisses his former mistress, Experience, who coolly observes, "Just like people, words develop illusions of grandeur."

Irigaray's commodities-among-themselves dance to their own composition and retire to burn nude on the beach. Caked with sand, an old woman reminds them about the price of their song, advising, "Remain indifferent when you go into the market to buy your tomatoes; no doubt they will be ripe. But if you go into the market, tell them you don't like the arrangement of their vegetable stalls, and then ask for your tomatoes. Beware, you'll find nothing but spoiled fruit."

Most learn this lesson well.

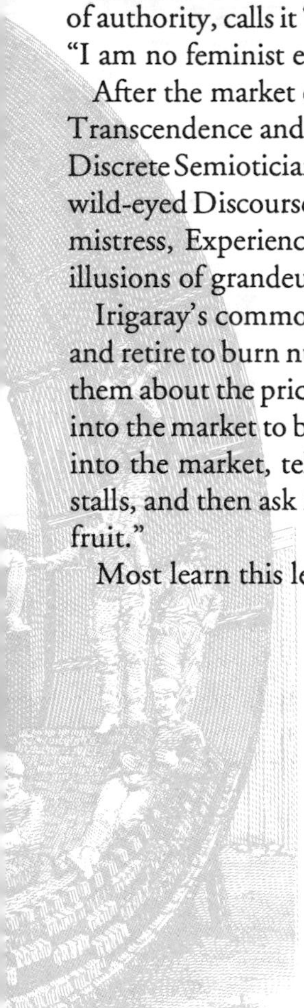

Fig. 75

At night, she dreams *tomate (f.) . . . her hand extended disappears beneath the platter this white porcelain oval layered Ah tomatoes sliced RED cut round how thin skinned they echo what was lost to us like tomatoes thought to be misnamed on a round-the-world voyage in seventeen hundred and seventy-seven when the final sound of a Spanish "tomate" exploded ending pushed ovoid made "tomato" strange fruit mistaken plum or pear sometimes called "loveapple" thought to have aphrodisiac properties now lost in this scarlet turn inside throated membranes our hearts' pebbled chambers the subject slips through her lips)*

At seven a.m., the long black car comes to pick her up; she thinks "Mercedes." Her lover gets out of bed. Refusing a ride, she might have put on her watch and walked home, feeling the strap loosen or the watch fall. Time out on the sidewalk. Later she says she would have stepped into her dream's Mercedes had it not been a hearse. As it was, her lover's "lost" watch was still on her bedside table as though retrieved by sleep.

The two women laugh as Mr. Het tips his hat from the black car and insists that "bad timing" is resistance and fear of heights. Before climbing into their sleep again, they rescript his lines into the strong but exceptionally silent type.

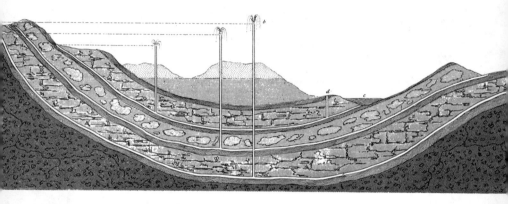

Fig. 76

Later a friendly conversation on the couch between literature and psychoanalysis where two women drift alongside their own mental tracks. Hang up memory. Her hand guides the pen into territory she has not set foot on other than in dream. The story went like this: two women drift in and out of friendly conversation tide out sand imprint of bare running feet towards a canoe (red of course) heading out to unknown islands or they stride toward forests map in hand filled in without compass south-west of nostalgia or they turn their back on recollection as it stirs to life in hands long enough to grip paddles arced prisms of water and light less memory than promise

the family romance heats up)

During Christmas dinner, they decline to attend midnight service, carve turkey, each other, in half. A distant relative in the military, on hearing another black woman has been shot dead, says (the swagger of pity in his voice), "It takes a lot of courage to pull the trigger." An older woman, filling up the silence, chimes into the spirit, wishing she had invested in Singer sewing machines when they manufactured armaments. Stocks soar without her.

Fig. 82

Wilhelm Reich's granddaughter had been in her second grade class. One day little Nora mentioned that her father spent all his mornings locked in the bathroom with his newspaper. She was certain there was something more to this story than met the eye. Were orgone tiles plastered over the bathroom walls? She couldn't be certain, though she often noted a flush in her student's cheeks.

he takes up where her tattoo leaves off)

Many years after she slashed her wrist, he blamed her for being the light of his
soul. This was not the self-serving version of her story. His impotence with her
had depended on the other woman identical to her in many respects, though
the intriguing gap in her rival's front teeth and full breasts inspired his other
illuminated name, "light of my body." That's how she remembered it — caught
between two women in the Aristotelian splits. One night she found a wet
razorblade in her right (write) hand, the left wrist held out, waiting. A gesture,
quick blue edges curl back, blood drips towards her fingertips, the nightgown,
wet with flowing, clings to her body, open in any animal's surprise.

Fig. 85

The next day, he leaves both of them high and dry. Who remembers his
handsome face, the temporary quicksilver tongue? How he cooked up expensive meat for one when they had no money. How he stole her letters, her words
hinged on the page for twenty years waiting for this stare.

1957 feminine écriture, in English)

Six years old, left-handed, she liked cabbage. Arms and legs spread out towards the four corners of the room, she was her father's airplane swirl of low flight patterns on the carpet. After a long boozy dinner, she flew higher, borne up by his sprung legs over the harvest-gold tweed sofa. Across the living room, descending, she brushed the hunting-scene curtains her sisters had set on fire last summer.

Time's up for any unwilling Icarus. Her wings crumple to the ground where she loudly reads the odd cavity in her wrist as pain. Her mother agrees temporarily. Four minutes later when the girl crosses the room towards her father, an imperceptible twist of her arm returns small bones to their places. Examining her wrist, no longer hollow with memory, her father pronounces, "There's nothing the matter." The girl cries to her mother who looks away, contemplating her lap. A moment later, recomposed, she explains to her weeping daughter, "Nothing, just a sprain. . . ."

(The delirium of identity makes it possible to imagine her wrist as opposed to any other wrist broken in play, or not. Pain and the lies of crumpled bodies sound hyperbolic truth. Another drunken fist hinges the bone.)

Later at the hospital, the girl's x-rays authorize the hair-line fracture cracked through the bone. In the absence of her parents, did she sign the release form with her right hand?

Fig. 91

Thirty years later at the conference, a writer offers this unpaid signatorial advice: *Fasten on your signature before you hit the decks. You might need it. Just in case, sew it into your pocket or the nape of your neck. Stitch up a little something on your left buttock in light of the others' stars and stripes, big-city or just plain big-fish insignia. Flash it from under a short skirt. Body language like this makes waves of spectatorial applause only sound like appropriation.*

Remove when dancing. Snip. Snip.

In this eventuality, *how do we tell us apart?*

the reader closes the book, touches up her make-up)

Her husband wanted her to sign the papers right away in case later she wanted what he wouldn't like to provide for her. Her lawyer told her, "You're a fool." She agreed and signed. That evening, after dinner, her husband chased her around the kitchen table. Around and around, until she ran out the back door into the night, losing her skirt as she scaled the neighbour's fence. In the morning, she and her husband, now composed, loaded up his car and their rental trailer for a trip north across the border to her new home. On the way, he took a "shortcut" along a different highway. The sun was on their backs, so she knew they were headed in the right direction. She dreamed about signing again her old familiar name that ended with "son." She refused to talk with him about his work. When he turned away from the wheel to complain of her silence, he pulled over to the side of the road. His cock exposed. He told her. If she didn't. Perform. Or abandon.

Five hours later they reached her new apartment. It was small so they fit only her bed and a small table into the single room, storing her dishes in the fireplace. A small round window streamed ruby light. He told her all she could do in that room was make love to other men. She did not lie.

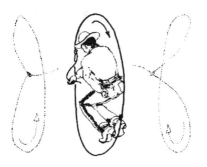

Fig. 94

Her earrings are too long to leave behind. The way the colour of everything turns feline stripped home. How this becomes T then is his and that too. How all the world spills into middle-of-the-street Spadina traffic; pedestrians glower, hung up on drugs. She likes to be liked but can't help that everyone treats her like yesterday's jesus. Speechless, she has no illusions, just effects. It all boils down to this. T kettle empty this and that nothing. Sporting pricey coordinated fashions called "new exceptional freedom to roam," she drives the full length of the country day and night stopping only at the loom of primary-coloured tourist sculptures. At Thunder Bay, the dreaming princess tempts her for weeks. Twelve-foot geese, fairy-tale mother's shoes and condo cowboys with hard-ons make irresistible parking-lot French toast.

signature. the key fits turning)

When they made love in the afternoon, his girlfriend languished in a sterile ward suffering from twentieth-century disease and reading under glass. This betrayal meant he would never "enter" her mistress body as though she were made fictive. Propped up, naked, tied to his iron bed, she would try to surprise him with yoga postures rarely displayed. Nonetheless, while she writhed quietly beyond his field of vision, he potted and sculpted his way across lofty cat-shit floors.

In the hospital during the early evening they often visit His Love. As though it were true, having not been spoken, they all chime in about the intimacy they shared. Sick with the world, His Love's gloved hands draw pictures of deflowered women and televisions snarled to a graphite tale.

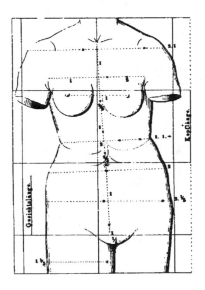

Fig. 99

Until the artist burned himself up in polka-dot effigy, his signature had been the chignon woven through the surface of the table stippled pink *faux*-marble with dolls. A portion of his remains are lacquered here and onto his fetish painting — her parting gift of a slender female nude, a cut-out airbrushed from *Penthouse.*

Practising her full lotus headstand, she talks to the wall about his dead misery. The female nude stretched across the canvas repeats herself: *My left hand reaching beyond the frame indicates that I am eating pine nuts because I am rich and cannot resist helping myself to myself. In 1978, my thighs were thick with almonds. I have never been thick with want.*

collaborating, reader and writer think of nothing)

In a neo-colonial hotel on a hot Nassau evening, they dined with the aging no-longer-drunk musical comedy star who was redecorating his house with rare wood-carved panels. The gentrified folly of his home echoed with the privilege of "Camelot," the refrain which zigzagged across the continent on his trail. Snapping at his heels, content to settle for an appendage of the great one, two women approached her in the washroom and asked her whether she was a movie star. "Which one?" she asked, curious. They couldn't remember, but they wanted her autograph "anyway." "Just in case."

That night she realized that simulating notoriety required a complete transformation of her character. She had to take herself as seriously as others would if they did. If she were no longer ignored, she had to keep up appearances and avoid sounding superficial. Later she would have to be perceived as experiencing the good time others accomplished. Would this day-labour require better pay? Would psychoanalysis work through her relation to failure and power? She wanted a good father to guide her. The famous actor man would promise to play a loved one returned from the dead. On a plastic beach chair, he did so convincingly. She felt herself fill up with love. Would he examine himself too carefully in the glare of her sunglasses?

Fig. 102

Unlike Virginia Woolf, i am not the least phlegmatic. Even though i refuse to smile on command, i have, they say, a rare though subterfuge personality. Call it "darkly veiled ironic wit." i prefer to watch all things unfold, even myself at this very moment when my fingers move across the page, my letters bursting liquid crystal blue brilliance. i spell out this call to you. i am writing writing myself into being as though there were no tomorrow to appeal to you dear reader. and you. and you. Tomorrow may not be the bright blue idea which brings us into being.

memorial service speaks volumes)

Inside the covers of all of the deceased director's Peter Handke books, there was no signature. However, on each page of *Self-Accusation* there were fine, numbered, fat HB-lead pencil lines under H's words. I read:

1 *I came into the world*
2 *I became*
3 *I moved*
4 *I moved my mouth*
5 *I saw*
6 *I looked I learned*
7 *I learned*
8 *I became the object of sentences*
9 *I said my name*
10 *I learned to be able*
11 *I lived in time*
12 *I was able to want something*
13 *I made myself*
14 *I was supposed to comply with rules*
15 *I became capable*
. . .
22 *I expressed myself*
23 *I expressed myself in movements*
24 *I signified*
. . .
38 *I did not regard the movement of my shadow as proof of the movement of the earth. I did not regard my fear of the dark as proof of the earth. I did not regard my fear of the dark as proof of my existence. I did not regard the demands of reason for immortality as proof of life after death. I did not regard my nausea at the thought of the future as proof of my nonexistence after death. I did not regard subsiding pain as proof of the passage of time. I did not regard my lust for life as proof that time stands still.*

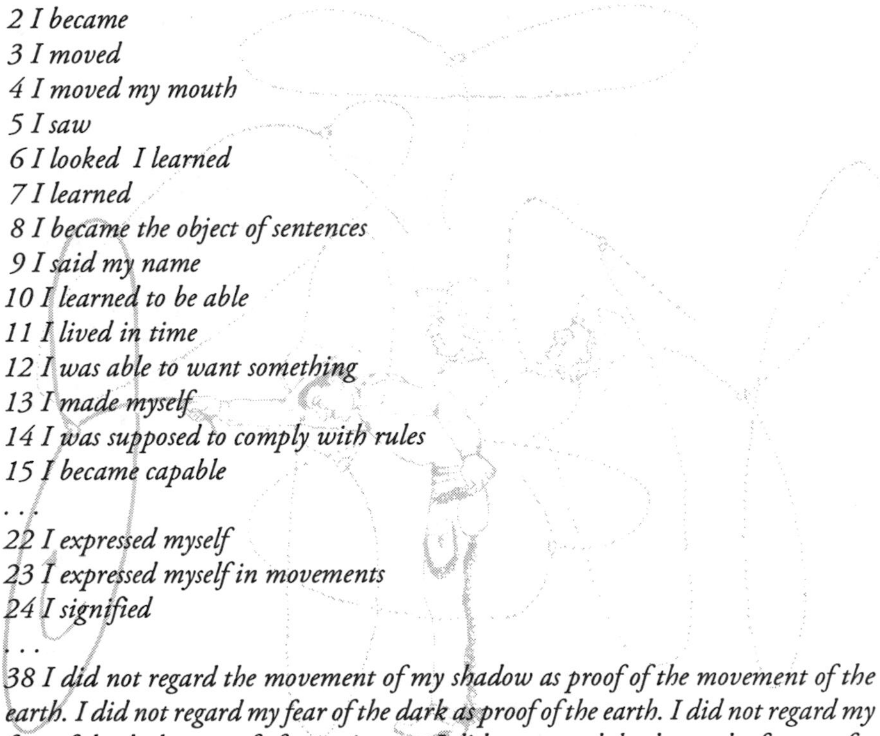

Fig. 107

Number 38 was not underlined but deserves quotation since as she read these words she remembered with love her dead friend; the director with the pencil had the same haircut as Peter Handke, the writer, who wrote number 40, *I went to the theatre*. Which he did.

she learns to look both ways)

Unearthed in an island jungle dig where Mayan ruins were once exposed, two jade beads made their way in his pocket to Pickering Jewellers. Pierced and linked with irregular gold nuggets, they became gifts for his daughter and his wife. One was lost at the drive-in, the other at Ghost Lake.

Every pebble looks alike along the shoulder of the road. A crack runs right up alongside the asphalt parallel to a white line (broken) running all the way to Banff. At one hundred and twenty kilometres per hour, the hood of the car rattles like wings taking off so I slow just in case. Out of the car, "Ghost Lake" sign to my right, car at my left, mountains focused in between. No problem, so we get back in the car and ... "Drive," she said all along the highway. Reaching down she notices her necklace, broken open, jade bead gone. Dangling brass beads drop off one by one.

Though February, it was almost hot walking along the roadside. Waiting for the jade bead to return to her hand from its resting place here or there, she sucked a stone, humming her song.

Fig. 111

He told her a loophole was an opening where small arms could be fired. It also permits observation. He let on there was a trick he had been meaning to teach her, but she was too slow to catch on. That's what he said and that's why he never did. That's why in the Cochrane bookstore filled with spirit-lines and winter count stories, she bought her own *Will Rogers Rope Tricks*.

Over the years she imagines she will appreciate the reversible qualities of knots. Her roping begins with the spin of a flat loop. She avoids "The Wedding Ring" and "The Butterfly" but eventually masters "The Reverse Ocean Wave." She hears that in Spanish the wave goes around to the right. On a good day here on the prairies, the rope balloons and floats in sun-dogs above her head, refusing Will's rope dream of a *perfect circle around an imaginary centre.*

excerpts from the journals of Alberta Borges

Whenever there is November in my soul
I seek out mild winters.
Eli Mandel

Alberta's Manual for Whestern Culture

Learn the horizon divides what is not.
Cotton onto margins.
Dress to kill self-dramatization at low cost.
Appreciate autumnal wet dreams.
Latch onto northern storyteller in concert.
Let your acreage ochre.
Grieve when your goin's gone.
Recollect in stages.
Live, a little.
Call your compass breathless.

Alberta Learns to Drive

Foothills crib the prairie, rim horizon's cup. Across hours, blue haze clouding . . .

Later, a bad dream pinch spins her compass to reverse. Not mountains but bookshelves tower, perpendicular and empty. In search of a story, Alberta spirals up a staircase and wonders where the books have gone. At 2001 metres, stretching onto the summit's smooth top, Alberta adjusts her glasses to clear light and contemplates the sheer shelfless drop into

Saskatchewan

Alberta Writes to Prairie Dog

Refuse the frozen lack. Revise blank hieroglyphs. Hold onto courtyard song, the clatter of porcelain voices. Circle your tongue in wagons.

Alberta

contemplates a death worse than fate: the North Saskatchewan in February.
River ice ruptured was
rift
edge

Alberta Meets Travelling Anna

Sing the ringing timber, cries Anna.
The sound of a woman's heart
Sing out the grief
Sing river

Alberta Visits Frank Kafka

He is ill: night sweats and chills during the day. She does not reach out to touch him when they talk of his "condition." She kisses the dark cancerous marks on his cheek. His lips miss hers. Hers . . .

Alberta Learns to Enjoy the Movies

Because she bored easily in Kin Kanyon? Behind the facade of prairie plain speech, vernacular stucco and ranch-levelled lives, epic criminal acts burn in winter kills. Every season, murder plots in corridors and streets are predictable only in naming the dead. Tragedy is popular. During natural feasts, public citizens parade neurotic agony under night dance shades
green skirts.

Alberta Analyses
Frank's Circumstantial Evidence

One doesn't jump to conclusions or slide into states of mind.
One doesn't contain anti-plain sentiment in words.
One doesn't wait for the parade.

Alberta Hears Nellie Dispense Advice

Listen while trees *feather-stitch the city,*
intones Nellie
finger the knotted lifeline,
the palm of my hand

Alberta Becomes Borgesian Director

Gossips circulate the flaccid underbelly of prejudice: judgement before corporeal fact. (Speculate on Alberta's sexual preference. Does she prefer honey oil
rubs or lathes?

Upside Down, Alberta Meditates

Her morbidity is not a pose. It is as sincere as she is herself. Swami Leduc says true power does not fuel enemies. Now that Alberta has enemies, she knows she is powerless. Her earnest enthusiasm and joy may not stand up to the cunning poised fingers, the unwashed blade at her back.

Alberta Dances in the Cowboy Bar

Reconsider urban life. All the girls in the cowboy bar dance with the cowboys' dream to straddle busting broncos. Tight blue jeans and white fringed boots two-step beside the bar. Floor-length sequins interrupt the proceedings. From farm to malled suburb in one fell swoop. No intermediate drift through urban streets to interrupt the shift from familial to familiar, neighbours to new neighbours. No city life with clanging cultures: sub-urban, not quite precise.

Alberta Takes a Trip
Beyond the Beyond of the Barren Land

At three thousand feet she resolves her desire for escape, dissolves her angst. Heady with oxygen deprivation, Alberta drifts towards a fertile valley. The balloon loses altitude, dumps her out in a former farmer's field. "Howdy," says the former farm woman. Alberta takes note of the friendly communitarian handshake and compares the rugged individualism of her home town.

Malice Reveals Her Cooties to Alberta

The guest speaker arrives in voluminous skirts and cowboy boots. Apologizing for her inability to speak comfortably in public, she proceeds to speak comfortably in public. She introduces the Professional Woman's Association to the trauma of her history: slings and arrows from homemaker to policy baker. Apologizing again for her inability to speak comfortably in public, she introduces her plan for the future.

"Let's," she proposes, "remake the establishment in my own image."

Alberta ponders vectors of refracted light.

Alberta Stares Right through Her

poof

Alberta Uncovers a Humanist Plot

Hang up the telephones of small men. A radical fringe group of intellectuals forms a liberal humanist splinter group. Transmission lines tremble with memos and memories of baseball. The Americans hole up in their provincial offices facing north to the river, plot to overthrow the government. Passionate outbursts from smokers rail against "those corrosive artsy craftsy lefties." The word *sailboat* blinks off/on in small circles before their eyes. Measurements indicate tiny tower shortages.

(Alberta and Frank caucus and muse: "Will spring nourish this insurrection or find it nodding off in March?"

Alberta Encounters the Second Circle of Hell

whipped frenzy of All-Season palm fronds

Alberta Meets Her Maker or Enters the Race

"Make no mistake. The critic is born to enliven the dead," intones the art critic Dr. Panofsky. Eminent judges gather to confer about the critical beauty contest. Invited international phrenologists adjudicate the first stage of the competition where head bumps indicate mental ruminations. "Just a tap, please," pleads the good doctor, silver hammer in hand. Competitors don't breathe a word — not a tremor or shiver, not even a jerk as he hits home to determine the truly plum cranial chamber. Deep thuds through the head lines echo Dr. Panofsky's progress. A chorus of rhythmic incantations (*play dead play dead*) is punctuated occasionally by the small high-pitched cries of disqualified subjects. Those who pass the Failure-to-Breathe test are removed on stretchers to the congeniality contest. Alberta revives to fail.

Dr. Panofsky Invokes the Mirror Stage

The final gruelling round of competition begins. Dr. Panofsky points towards the hyperbolic looking glass and loses himself for a moment in the splendid gilt swirls of his fame. The finalists, male and motionless, are wheeled towards the mirror. Alberta catches her breath. Back and forth in the delirium of the moment, judges sway to their triumphant song: "O twinned soul, beard of beards. O dead son of returned sons of resurrected father. O more of the same . . ." A magic circle of identical forms fills the room with haunting cries of loon. Dr. Panofsky collapses in the bliss of recognition.

Alberta Eats Crow

Clean, pluck, bind and truss the bird.
Bake. Prick. Baste. Serve.

Alberta Studies Gender Construction

Frank says a schizophrenic is lost in inner space. "In conversation, I misjudge the source of your voice, speak in error into your eye."

"Can we turn your theory inside out?" asks Alberta. "Can we hypothesize that anti-feminists are lost in outer space? Darkly diminished heroes in their own minds, they read woman as betrayal, female collectivity as blind ambition. At loose spatial ends, do they mistake the queen for the feminine, the girl for their heart?"

The Youth Revolution Preaches to Alberta

Aspire to diamond ring and bungalow, baby pink and blue.
Monitor vertical planes.
Drive home safely.
Smash through born-again static in preparation for war.
Keep your TV tuned to revelations.

Illuminated Alberta

gold-leaf home care

Alberta Reads a Northern Bestseller on Solitude

The author recommends repair over despair, cites the solitudinous lives of many unhappy artists and writers. The author, an avid sportsman, recommends the reader follow in the footsteps of the cultural greats. "Repair yourself through masterpieces," he advises. In spite of everything, he continues, "If you lack talent and commitment, take the path of least resistance: canoe with a companion."

Alberta Searches for Oppositional Culture

Alberta Breeds
a Story within a Story

Ghost town openings board up even though memory paints coal dust aquamarine or peach. Arctic winds rattle shut expectations. Under the *Cadomin Studio* green neon, the leading man (movie-idol-white-man-in-masquerade-as-the-Chief) mysteriously dies. No funeral is arranged. Considering a cast of none, the director steps in front of the camera to become split-screen celluloid twins who play themselves. "Alberta made 'er," he says to Hollywood agents, "she's a looker." In the Legion, carved   jesus   wood   tacked   door to door left stragglers sludge nostalgia's wing brush thud transparent tone au verso music terror of walls

Alberta Investigates Transformation

Looks for a gun. Army and Navy sells ammunition on demand. Save your expert witnesses, bestsellers and alibis. Larch trees trace the perimeter of the acreage: two resident philosophers beat time to the wind. Air pulsates across the prairie from another source: strange atonal sheep-herding songs of a single male voice. Three figures lurch into view, triggers moist with sweat. Will something more wholesome than a Cartesian split occur?

Alberta Chants "MY WILD BODY IS A CORPSE"
(after Wilfred Watson)

My body is dead. Dead. Dead. My body is dead and the mouth that was breathes in radio air humours confused with sound grain the matter no more than this hand moving fingers pianissimo across the keyboard the sound of one hand's right hand work the source of what's left. *knock knock* The remainder dead yet the sound of your wild corpse spinning wheels through spinster bobbins. My wild body is a corpse I say, touching myself in places never yours. This, no declaration of independence, is complicity: yours, mine, these propositions of wild stand in for something like my body spirit. Dead yet your "my wild"

Alberta Meets Her Mentor

The Old Woman In Floral Print writes oedipal when she isn't planning local implosions. Walls stand up under stress so all it takes, she says, is the long poem or a well-thumbed *Blaster's Handbook*. A small rainy commotion on the third floor brings out the worms. No one is killed in the seduction of backlash. Watch the tumble in time.

Alberta Reads Strange Sisters

... desire and torment swept through Joyce's trembling young body at the gentle touch of Edith's cool hand upon her ... Could she free herself from Louise's kind of love? ... both were indescribably lovely ... yet one wanted a man's love ... while the other craved a ... revealingly frank novel of women who love women because they fear to love men ...

desire   who   love   and   torment women   at   free   herself   wanted

trembling   the other   hand   herself   love   a   man's   other   she

touch   cool   joy   upon   could   kind   of   indescribably   ith   yet

one   through   and   swept   lovely   frank   ovel   because   to   bab

love   craved   ably   ingly   ing   ouise   while   the   revealing   ly

Alberta's Ear: Radio Olympic Lake

On the airwaves, politicians tight in small rooms quote Mao and shop for bargains in the same breath. It's gonna blow, they say after the first night. It's almost a winner, they gloat after the fourth. On the evening of the fifth, they rush through a women's chorus of the satisfaction song they can't hear. By the evening of the sixth, from east to west, everyone hangs up when they remember to call home. A few days later, Chief Chin, the only one they can see, waves them into his ring of silence. Splinters are on their minds; finger-tapping tortures that purple your nail.

Alberta Watches the Chin's Epic

In response, sharp-eyed showmen capitalize on the new grandstand. To add to the drama, the script calls for The Chin's outfit to lose a front wheel, then the box and, in a dramatic finale, the hind wheels. While the wagon disintegrates, Get-Even leaps onto the wheel team like a Roman racer.

Alberta muses from the sidelines, "Not everyone survives the main event."

Alberta Borges Visits West Coast Islanders

Suffers bloat in the rain. "Keep falling," Alberta croons at night, "so I'll know who I am." The only scary wildness she finds is the raccoon treed in cherries by Prairie Dog who waits for grazing bucks before his solitary business.

By nightfall, double-headed Amazonian implements have chopped up dinner for twelve. "This may not be bucking country but I feel safe here without my reins," Alberta sighs into the radio. Under a waxing moon, the only beasts through her windows free-float like swallows.

Alberta Skims along the Surface of Things

opium kayaks sticky heat rolled in hand rimbaud clouds of cedar forest arc red
of waxwing pomegranate sculls not far behind silly laughter from juice box to
seal's O of whiskered   sweet chill of her closes into dark-eyed splash

Alberta Restores the Sound of Dishes

The mess inside pearl sludge makes sense like dew. If she talks about the sheen,
the texture between her teeth drops out of the picture. If she worries the taste,
the touch drifts far away.
  "Catch the dream," says her TV.
  Painting waves of blue across her window, Alberta cries,
  "Like this? ((((((((((((((((((((((((((((((((((((
  ((((((((((((((((((((((((((((((
      (((((((((((((((((((((((((((
  (((((((((((((((((((((((((((
  (((((((((((((
  (((((((((((((((((((((((((((((((((((((
  (((((((((((((((((((((((((((
    (((((((((((((((((
  (((((((((((((((((((((((

  ((((((((((mollusc heart
  aprons hair (((((((((((
  ((((((((((((((((((((tip long line up
  (((((((
      (((((((((((((((((((((((((((((
  ((high-rise moss   ((intensity

Alberta Shops for Disciplined Knowledge

"Home is where the art is," Alberta urges lamps and fellow shoppers. "*Cui bono?*" replies Frank who expects no answer from The Sandwichmen of West Edmonton Mall who advertise veiled discipline to street-walker and cultural critic alike. No longer the spring line, their cooked books are on special. Alberta compares goods, tracing the thread everywhere along brass-handled corridors. "Follow me anywhere," she beckons to Prairie Dog who noses the ground and does. Frank, less exuberant, dodges The Thin Sandwichman, dismissing his propaganda as "spreading it too thin."

Alberta Investigates Ellipses

. . . the gap protects her from the failure of what she doesn't want to know. Happily, space leaves her open to criticism, not demonization. "Is clarity a form of cruelty or an intimation of flatness?" Alberta consults The Iceberg Lady's journal for a clue. In her voice which envelops failure, deep sounding middles never dive towards the same story twice.

"Emma! Emma! Be frank," Alberta writes in a panic to her Dauphin friend. "Is it true you no longer love me? Tell me the story I want to hear." In reply, Emma sends her no note with the massage in a suitcase she knows will stretch out Alberta's anxious limbs.

Who will untangle her mind?

Alberta Studies Snaps of Clam Shucker

Summer breeze coast to coast across the graveyard stoned Atlantic mauve horizon slips by in spite of their dream. No sleep past this crack cold dawn when words wake everywhere the wallpaper. Clam Shucker writes man/fish poems and tries to keep his head. Conversational tears mean insight. Heigh-ho smoke falls in the woodshed where Alberta laments her salmon song without cowboys. "That's not the whole story," sighs Alberta. Her pen listens for Clam Shucker's trick, minding verbs *pocket* and *reply*.

Alberta Corners Flocks of Birds

How they fill the empty sky. Thrill to the sparrow. Nine crested ringed jays ruffle up the pine. (The brrrrrrrrr of wings.) "Bring me my blue," calls the magpie. Grit the belly of the bird swung low. Chatter begins in earnest through the pane. Eyes bead blind behind the whiteness.

Look. Alberta writes.

TV Teaches Alberta the Meaning of the Words

to right ink makes mustard gas this boy 1917 lung up spume of yellow ribbons till home sweet sister tied like verb to enter stopped up uncut rooms scrub again this and these words hooked rub selling AAGGHHH everywhere blow one house on top of another no basement of history to worry bodies hung up like *boeuf* roped interruption she says she feels dead no fight left to act no requirement quit ahead with smart bombs foolish choices a gas boy 1917 history's auxiliary insurance presentiment of no tomorrow she breathes

Alberta Hears SINGER Sewing Machines

and the bulb in her desk lamp by GEE EEE declares war in a night sky of *fireworks* the scream of *sirens* announce *the tail on that one!* Alberta settles onto her windowledge, the carpet of everyday explosives brought to you by HOOVER. Our Man Joe from High River stands on the doorjamb shouting *give peace a chance.* A peace=war=peace=war rhythm lines longer than a sixty-second spot howl of projected figures:

What comes after twenty-six?
One?
Oh.
What comes after one hundred thousand?
Three hundred thousand?

Miami
May 1, 1991

Dear Frank

Outriders are a sombre lot. With the intestinal fortitude and dust of lean bull-riders, they are not the jockeys we need. At the hotel on the road, all the dead animals in the "Indian Room" were shot by the proprietor. Tonight forest fires circle around us out of control. In this tough scene, imagine your quick recovery.

Yours as ever

Albnth

Domestic
Accounts

A Family Holiday in Sunny Puerto Plata

Undeniable "natives" include the soursop, star apple, cashew, wild guava, wild pepper, mahogany, logwood amapola, satinwood, frangipani, calabash, royal palm, agave, and long leaf pine. . . . Coconut, mango, rose apple, organ cactus, and almond from India and the East Indies; bread-fruit from the South Pacific; eucalyptus from Australia; flamboyants, castor-oil plants, and coffee plants from Africa; hibiscus from Asia; bougainvillaea from Brazil; poinsettia from Central America; white angel's trumpet from Peru; cocoa from Mexico; papayas and limes from Venezuela. . . . The Indians themselves are believed to have brought with them from the South American mainland bananas, sweet potatoes, peanuts, and their staple food, the starchy manioc root.

Selden Rodman

Domination is a twisting of the bonds of love. . . .

I'm somewhere with my family in the Dominican Republic down the long beach from Cristobal Colón's first landing. This is the new world dancing in the streets to merengue music; tin drum harps and accordions strike up the bands. A Black man on the beach tells how the White man's dogs are "classist" because they bark at all black men who pass through the surf at their territory's end. After the American invasion of 1965, the street graffiti read, "Junkies go home."

. . . Domination does not . . .

In the beautifully landscaped and very cheap seaside resort, the Anglo and Italian-Canadian investors congregate in the dining room suspended over a lily and mosquito-infested pool for their welcome orientation and Bloody Caesars. *. . . bounded on the north by the Atlantic Ocean, on the south by the Caribbean Sea, and on the west by the Republic of Haiti. . . .*
During the talk, they are told about the lizards, the cockroaches, the leaky roof, the undercurrents, the poor electricity, the rain, the thieves, the concept of time, the undertow, the motorcycle accidents, the bad drivers, the potholes, the poor countryside, the beggars, the lying money-changers. All this at 11:00 Christmas morning.

. . . repress the desire for recognition; . . .

I am not the only one wearing my Leonard Cohen concert t-shirt of a mustard-coloured Leonard Cohen look-alike banana-eater. On the beach, little boys run for pina coladas carved out of whole fresh pineapples, shuck a dozen oysters for two dollars, bring you the change before they pocket it inside torn trousers, before they tilt their plywood boards toward the afternoon surf. On the beach, four young boys sculpt sunbathers in the sand. The male figure's long thick penis sticks straight up in the air; seaweed stands in for the female body's pubic hair, her vagina bored out by probing fingers whenever a bikini-clad woman walks by. On the beach, there is a man wearing his Leonard Cohen t-shirt with mustard-coloured banana-eater. He is not Leonard Cohen: too tall and no sun-glasses on a hot afternoon; no women at his large feet.

. . . rather, it enlists and transforms it. . . .

The dining room photograph contains (as in vase) the florid faces of the family: five men, two women. Sun and good health thrill their cheeks as they lean across the table towards the photographer, a Frenchman who has been here for seventeen years photographing invasions and christenings, funerals and conventions. Dressed all in white, he takes two photographs: both are identical in everything except their blinking eyes — off/on lidded looks glance towards the camera.

. . . Domination does not . . .

Standing on the roadway dodging motorbikes and small cars dodging the potholes, two Black women, waitresses at the resort, wait for a bus to pick them up. Two pesos for the pleasure of a van rocking with bodies out the door. A White man stops his car and beckons to the White tourists who slide into their seats and begin their tourist conversation. "How long you been here? . . . Where you from? . . . How d'ya like it?" All this a prelude to the delivery of this monologue as they pass through hills of waving pampas grass: "The seven years I been here are seven years too long. I got my ideas bout what we gotta do here, the only thing we oughta do here, what we shoudda done here, just like we done in the Pacific: drop one of em big A-bombs on this whole island. People here lie cheat steal. That's all they're good for. You know — I'm a contractor here just like I was back home in Wisconsin and just last month I lost the engine out of my front-end loader. You know how big that engine was — BIG as this truck. No surprise to me: people here steal anything that isn't tied down. You know where the Bible talks about slavery, well this here is the place for it. Ship all these Dominican people over to the States as slaves. Just take over this place and really run it. It was only forty years ago here in Sosua that a German took a hundred Jews for a long walk on this same road we're drivin down. Not forty years ago. Yep. If I was you I'd go home and get forty guns and load em and put em in the corner and tell my children if they touch em you'll break their fingers and then I'd just sit there and wait for em to come to git you."

. . . repress the desire for recognition. . . .

Wait for him to come and get you.

Get you. Right there with your broken fingers where he beat you with the hot noontime scream butt end of his rifle just before the whole village rises up in the dead of night with wrenches and silent machinery to unhinge this white man's engine to toss it into the sea to drift to rest on Spanish amphorae spilling rich oils for thirteenth-century feasts.

. . . The devaluation of the mother that inevitably accompanies . . .

The conversation goes something like this without sentences the mother and daughter love each other without doubt as though it mattered these two women no different from others stare silent into photographs as though words didn't matter each tells the other secretly how it might be if they could only tear their eyes away hear words inside photographs of brides the mother's pearled satin flounces blonde '40s hair waves to the tilt of aqua-feathered hats on small town prairie church steps towards the younger '60s fashionable iconoclast daughter crushes her rose chiffon dress poses against a pool's chain-link fence her at-home-wedding attire designed by a Black American so long she stumbles down the hill on her way to the secular willow grove ceremony a clearing in fact completely inside one another how could they see anything from this place of belonging this motherly daughterly talk the mother asks dear what is the matter? the daughter petulant says nothing turns her head towards the floral bedspread the fan above whirls slow her words say the way family dinner voices talk over her she the only girl getting a word in edgewise there being silence beyond this except angular expletives finally the source of her own ambition the mother she says the bad role model though role model doesn't add up to mother but still there she sits between fish and chips fudges again erases herself mid-conversation convenient hiatus just as all the boys heat up their exchange the girls now just that and quiet or else invisible girl tongues wag inside girl heads their eyes unblemished screens of tabled thought.

. . . the idealization of the father, however, . . .

In the neighbouring town of Sosua, a synagogue stands on a cliff by the beach. The dark-skinned Jewish man in his t-shirt store Goin Bananas tells me this business is the beginning of his empire. Though he "could have gone to medical school," he now owns the new shopping mall, part of what was once land parcel number 147. He tells his story: how the dictator Trujillo's one big foreign blunder dictated his own family history. In 1937, rumours circulate that Trujillo is foiled in his attempt to take over neighbouring Haiti. This is the only perverse rationale he could have used to justify his massacre of Haitian migrant workers: *cut down by rifles, thrown to crocodiles, rounded up in stockades, chopped up with machetes* — one Haitian maid stabbed with the carving knife as she served the roast. In order to clear his name of these atrocities internationally, Trujillo announced that he would let one hundred thousand German Jews into the country. In order to whiten the Dominican race, he demands that ninety thousand are eligible bachelors.

. . . gives the father's role as liberator . . .

A Sosua father's testimony: "One hundred and sixty families remain out of the total of five hundred to six hundred families that came here. A somewhat larger number of Spanish Republicans came at the same time, but proving to be a political liability they were not treated well, and most of them re-emigrated to Mexico. Those of us who stayed prospered with our cheese and sausage cooperatives at Sosua. What did it all prove? Trujillo needed ambassadors of goodwill. Tired of politics and persecution abroad, we Jews complied. He used us. He used me. After all, he had done nothing but good things for us. Like the others I didn't believe in the tales of murder and corruption at first. Why, just a year before his death he came unannounced to a service at our synagogue. There he sat, gazing raptly at the Torah for two hours. After the service he mingled freely with us, slapping us heartily on the back and joking. 'Can I have a visa for Israel?' he asked me. 'Why not, your Excellency?' 'Ah! Don't be so quick. Don't forget I'm the good friend of Nasser!' (roars of laughter). So he was our friend. Hadn't he given us $60,000 for our synagogue? So we told people how maligned he was by Communist propaganda. Just as the 'good Germans' had kept their eyes closed to the extermination of our people in the Death Camps, which they had 'never heard of,' so we kept our eyes closed. We saw no evil. We heard no evil. We did well. We made money. Even when neighbours disappeared, we didn't notice — or attributed their disappearance to natural causes. We noticed nothing unusual. We didn't want to."

. . . a special twist for women. . . .

"The sign over the lunatic asylum at Nigua — 'We owe everything to Trujillo.' "

. . . It means that their necessary identification . . .

In the violet mountains above the sea, they ride towards a grotto. Her horse is called Ariadne. She swears this is true. Purple iodine marks a wound the tattered leather halter has eaten through her flesh: Ariadne is in pain. En route, the rains fall through forests; oranges, lemons fall into their arms; horses' hooves fall in a careening gallop toward a warm turquoise mountain stream where the guide will reappear a half hour after their arrival — reappear; that is, resurface from the bottom of the stream and, without a word, beckon them to swim into the cave pulsating with candles illuminating the inner mountain stream. She swims with her brothers who call out to ghosts, to mountain men and mysterious lingerers who line rock walls. She swims with her brothers now disappeared for too long under water and the mountain which tends toward the light.

. . . with their mothers, with existing femininity . . .

All this grotto and tropical fruit and no Alain Delon naked beside his yellow Rolls Royce. All this she saw in the movies with her fourteen-year-old fellow girl campers who sat with hands clasped in laps, knees crossed tightly. At the end of the film, Alain Delon's white body flickers in their eyes as they rush forward armed with Coca-Cola to extinguish the third-row cigarette fire smouldering in the empty seat. No other tropical memory of water and heat comes to mind other than the splendid waterfall scene spotted from her bedroom window night after night through winter trees on the drive-in screen. In this movie, the unmarried pregnant woman was righteously punished for her crime, her splendour in the grass. This latter humiliation resurfaces as dim memory since she always fell asleep before the retribution scene.

. . . is likely to subvert . . .

Who would return to this land of rain and real estate speculators, Toronto suburbanites or the little Québec perched on the hills beside the windsurf capital of the Caribbean? Did they/she care in the listless heat of a single sun-blasted afternoon?

In the end, the isolation of the resort makes her feel crazy with boredom, a bourgeois habit and one she cannot overcome. She is crazy with boredom, as though a different setting might help. As though a different setting might help, she reads another book. She reads another book and recognizes a friend who has written well. She recognizes a friend who has written it, well, once a friend, always recognizable. Once a friend, always recognizable contours of memory list toward the bottom of a page. Recognizable contours of memory list toward the bottom of the page, catalogue her fears. Catalogue her fears at bottom you will find in the end she feels herself crazy with boredom.

. . . their struggle for independence. . . .

In kiosks along the beach, vendors hawk their wares: t-shirts with wind surfers and palm trees; beads and seashells; paintings and wood carvings. A favourite is the handkerchief-wrapped bust of a Black Dominican woman: these very women inspire the graffiti of Montreal Haitians who caution Canadian tourists against visiting the country where migrant Haitians live in misery.

In their Santo Domingo studio, brother and sister, Roxanne and Edison, paint up sculptures of Dominican women in swirls and surreal colours. Are they for the indiscriminate eye of the tourist or, more strategically, their dollars? One Black woman's face shines with startling elaborate red tattoos, her hair a fiery pink plume. Another figure, in stained-glass sea-foam tints, wraps tendrils of underwater life around her throat.

. . . The idealization of motherhood, which can be found in both . . .

In Caballeros Bar overlooking Sosua Bay, in a hotel favoured by German charters, the German film distributor, a feminist who speaks a half-dozen languages and has soft blonde skin, names the famous German film directors they have known. They speak in simple sentences and remember the American films of Wim Wenders and Herzog — the dozens of pairs of shoes in *Paris, Texas* which trace the new frontier horizon: a shoddy fetishized romance of the new world. The German woman tells how she went to the vault to fetch her valuables with the German Jewish hotelier who motioned toward a pistol on the shelf with this explanation: "I am ready if they ever decide to come and get me again."

The German woman admits sheepishly she knows nothing of Canada. "Does it exist?" the Canadian woman asks herself out loud, or has it signed itself over and out? The two women complain about their family Christmases, yearning to condense domestic interludes of silence and misrecognition. The German woman tells of her father in his village to the north of Munich where she lives. He is a living dead man, his leg amputated just before the war's end: no more marines, just a pension and memories. "He still believes he lives in the Third Reich. He still believes the lies."

. . . anti-feminist and feminist cultural politics, is an attempt to . . .

There must be more: her stepfather's withdrawal and silence when she tells him peevishly that she is bored. As though he will punish her with a refusal to communicate in the event that she might find it entertaining and thus disappoint her commitment to temporary misery.

. . . redeem woman's sphere of influence by idealizing . . .

As a child she remembered her room, how it had once been a dining room with a pass-through in the wall covered over with a plywood insert where she could hear kitchen conversations. At night, she masturbated, stifling sighs or moans of pleasure in case anyone was listening through the refrigerator: their hands fill with milk and bananas; ears press against coils of liquid gas.

. . . woman's sexualization and lack of agency. . . .

All week between the bar and the beach, she lies in bed surrounded outside by two brothers and two stepbrothers, a mother and a stepfather, the ideal nuclear family. She reads *The Bonds of Love* and nods her head in recognition. Still she takes part in the family romance: a fight breaks out and when she least suspects she tumbles into the free for all. No referee; no score. After the tidal wave, battered bodies brush off the sand, attempt a painless recovery of the equilibrium they imagine themselves to possess. There are no life jackets to preserve this illusion. Surf batters on no matter the conversation or conversion.

. . . This attitude toward sexuality preserves the old gender system, . . .

Neptune bears his trident out of the sea at Puerto Plata, not flat, but rich, the sign of Cristobal Colón's arrival on January 9, 1493. "The Indians' hair was worn long and tied in a bunch at the back of the crown of the head, giving an effect 'as the women of Spain wear it.' Plumes of parrot feathers and other birds were inserted." Colón records in his journal his meeting with Indians in what would become Haiti: "They bear no arms, and are all unprotected and so very cowardly that a thousand would not face three; so they are fit to be ordered about and made to work."

. . . so that freedom and desire remain an unchallenged male domain, . . .

On this island the Indians called Quisqueya, the "sailors had captured an Indian girl whose only adornment was a golden noseplug; it was a token that this island promised more than Cuba." *Some were mutilated and murdered, others killed themselves with cassava poison; routed from their land, many died of starvation and illness. Of the high estimate of three million Tainos Indians indigenous to the island in 1492, fifty thousand survived by 1508. By 1548, a Spanish historian estimated that no more than five hundred remained.*

. . . leaving women to be righteous but . . .

Zorro's exotic TV slash follows her this far south: the matador's hat, his sweep of cape and storm. All this a borrowed metaphor for longing. In Spanish, she says, "a little only a little." "Little, scanty, small, short (time)."

. . . de-eroticized, intimate and . . .

In the bar, she is too drunk to focus on the men who are bargaining with her brothers for her body. The men are serious, though the brothers later claim they are not. Oblivious to this fine economy, she dances with a prostitute in short, red skirt and herringbone tweed vest whose red lips open under the moonlight into a generous smile. Dancing close up now, they lose sight of the others and swirl arm in arm, the courtyard air fresh with the glitter of celestial ballroom stars. In her room alone later, she remembers the touch of her hands, fingertips thick with mothering and day labour.

. . . caring but pleasureless. . . .

In her dictionary a man and a woman wrap their fingers around their thumbs and brandish their fists toward us. In Spanish they find themselves named differently: his, a *puñado m. fistful, handful* (of dollars?); hers, a *puñada f. punch, blow* (me up down and away).

. . . And it fails to understand . . .

It is 2:20 and she has seduced the reader awake for a few moments before she closes the book and returns to sleep. The surf spills over with dark bodies spun out in waves. This is how she reads in the middle of her life, sucking in words like lungs.

. . . the underlying force of desire . . .

The trident bears three points: the sign of the father, the father of the father, the son; perhaps the son's son is skewered on the end. This is the place of the fathers, the drowned one washed up on the beach pierced by a coral tine.

. . . that ratifies male power, the adoration . . .

At the bottom, her watch undoes itself at her wrist's end, arrested at the time she left in the north-west. Now she drifts in and out of sleep in a tropical rain wind storm. This might be a hurricane so she awakens only to spot Aurora's arrival on the sea. Neptune's trident digs into her side — at at at.

. . . that helps create it ever anew.

Of women and fish

for Ntosake Shange and Phyllis Webb

For those whose fathers considered suicide only to drown
there is no consolation

For those whose fathers considered suicide
a husband in his image waits in the wings

For those whose fathers considered suicide only to drown
consider other factors

For those whose fathers commit suicide
Sartre confirms your despair

For those whose fathers commit suicide — the memory
terror of the beach
alone the knowledge of expansive sea turquoise to touch
the thigh the chest the breath the work
to be done to the death

For those whose fathers commit suicide
the fear for others the brothers
perhaps the mother

For those whose fathers considered suicide — a graph
blizzards circling say over saskatoon
writing farewell letters
gridded fantasies of sudden death

For those whose fathers considered suicide
a look
I love you runs relays in his circles of pain

For those whose fathers considered suicide
loathsome abandonment
swollen pulp, powdered flesh

For those whose fathers commit suicide
the urge to confess
your hatred at his flight

For those whose fathers commit suicide
the years
how could he have done such a thing

For those whose fathers commit suicide
the outrage
being outdone undone stood up till your dying day

For those whose fathers considered suicide
no kamikaze culture
enfolds your horror

For those whose fathers commit suicide
all-women's combat
troop drives

For those whose fathers consider suicide and drown
nightmares trapped in TV movies
the barroom aquariums
the one-piece suits

For those whose fathers commit suicide
no musical comedy nothing
like a dame

For those whose fathers commit suicide
ten years precede this writing

For those whose fathers considered suicide
attend to this detail
the other woman sharing this history sided with the other side

For those whose fathers consider suicide and drown
there is never a doubt

For those whose fathers considered suicide the submarine
becomes your dreamscape

For those whose fathers suicide and drown
the sharp bite of memory gives agony, gives vent to agony

For those whose fathers considered suicide
the manic ride out in the bay singing

For those whose fathers committed suicide
a strength resists
though all the weapons are in place

For those whose fathers commit suicide
an open book
the unfinished reading

on the couch

for vivien smith

a residue of fingerprints forms a water line above the couch where others absentminded or possibly with great concentration imagine their escape touch the wall sometimes in the feminine they wear bourgeois minks who tell their own stories sometimes they dress just like men in beards and galoshes look suspicious like the time they conspired to murder i swear before their escape before their sweating fingers wrestled free the speck of paint from the wall

perforated holes of ceiling tiles memorized then rearranged to secret patterns of seeing the eyes remember punctured openings of needles and pins or broken glass is this the way to dream?

fair weather fancy flight finger wishing fish swimswim upsuptwinsup in the sea the sea mother's body hidden in the breast baby suck in light breast bone sunk in flesh fat with flowing yes flowing in the bath bathe body boom (under water) held at head kicking mother's silence held in wardrobe hanging in closet blouse skirt scary under thing with wires (excrete the baby feeling) mother's shoes her pumps heels helicoptering through grass spinning out calves her ankle

so how do you do it day after day? i mean politically how do you do it? i mean how do you find the time? the money? is it worth it? what about body work? what about something quick and sweet?

the doctor leaves on schedule on vacation and this view framed by her picture window cuts away from snowy rooftop to tropical locale where i know i am in for it (cheap visual pun the turquoise sea tinting higher and higher   fish kisses on the pane

(primal scenes often are formally self-reflexive mucky photographs of open doors a peek that sticks to your hand h.d. saw writing on the wall everywhere didn't have to look at the old man's gruesome jaw called him *victorious mouth or voice or utterance* after his name walked daily to her *blameless physician* through the autumnal snow of swastikas: *it was vienna 1933*

remember the look down the stairway a look that remembers the silent moment of return *where's the baby?* i ask where's the baby born in a body made different dying at birth sister dead sister love the same though in different sister hoods identical or other swinging in a summertime where's the big bad wolf? is he coming? she's swinging out the window slight figure in the distance   will he choose or lose or where's the bad wolf?

the feminists have taken freud to the third world where he's up to no good. in masringo, zimbabwe, they take him to all-night parties where he refuses to dance, and naps under the table at three a.m. one day he steals batteries for his ghetto blaster. it isn't the first time, so they exile him to djenne, mali. all day long freud sleeps on mats reserved for the elders, ignores the mosque, secrets his abominable reputation. but word gets around. appalled, the elders ship him to mozambique. freud's portuguese may be passable in maputo, but he is impossible. concerned only with his personal comfort, he defies restrictions. non-stop complaints about air travel. says he prefers the open road, the train, in spite of ambushes. in desperation the feminists take him to the *all-china women's federation* in beijing for re-education. he takes a chill, dreams of the tropics he's lost, hallucinates the grey city as the labrador coast, dies at sea.

the bad sisters from the feminist collective meet the big daddies at avenue road and saint clair   the big daddies illustrate the phallus penis joke lower their pants the punch line barely visible   there's no moon on the dusty road there's trouble there's a shootout   their pants were down roland barthes looks like barthes   beautiful   though he plays thackeray in a french movie   *psychoanalysis* writes barthes *has a limited image repertoire* stories told over and middle begins again ending *sans fin*

really there is no air you can tell by the voice deep in hollows the current ringing syllables through your body your own voice spelled out in front of where you lie head tilted back *never trust a hemlock an inch above your mouth* cautioned mary butts your words breathe stutter to speech plea memory break on the listening chair the dogs and horses too in dreams but aren't they expensive? don't they have a price? the dogs and horses dogs in dream sound not at all a different movement of light on the wall falls through morning sun blinds moves into view on the couch trembling breath listens and further through to a cry slivers shadows on the floor under pressure of being in the room the being a dreaming remember she swings out the window slight figure in the distance she's swinging out the window there's light

Fundamental Rule

Rule which structures the analytic situation: the analysand is asked to say nothing and omit nothing from what comes into his mind, even where this seems to him unpleasant to have to communicate, ridiculous, devoid of interest or irrelevant.
Laplanche and Pontalis

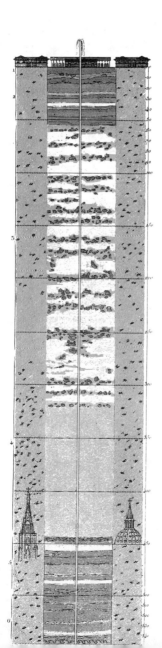

JUNE   "Men seldom make passes at girls who wear glasses."
   Adjusting your special analytic glasses, you hope this to be true. These glasses have six lenses. Two of them very major, very thick, where glasses usually face. In addition, two pairs of appendages fly like wings out beyond the ears. This quartet of symmetrical lenses, concave and convex, form specular cavities where vision is interior, the body transparent like ice.

SEPTEMBER   You have an inborn hostility toward men.
         You withdraw from the term "narcissistic."
         You want more than a twelve-year "relationship."
         You want your own pleasure now.
         No. Though I refused to recognize hostility, I now acknowledge it and imagine it less innate. No longer denied, I position it. Fill out the form: name, address, telephone, social insurance, father's name, mother's name, education, employment, awards, associations. I push it back across the table and listen to your language of assessment: "You have an inborn hostility toward men."

OCTOBER   "Mannequins have to take abuse from the public, who like to touch them. It seems to be quite a joke to remove arms and hands."

MARCH   Saint Paul said, "Rather marry than burn." I say, "*Mary* and burn." I dream I meet my husband after a long separation. I never learn, he talks me into it, and there I am terrified again in my own house, running down the stairs, keys in hand, shoes in hand. Running down the stairs, twenty dollars in hand. He, in sky blue vest, is chasing me. Out on the street like a nineteenth-century engraving: all the cop cars full up. Catatonics. Pimps galore. I run to find a streetcar, a subway, a cop. Look! The husband runs past fast not recognizing me. Smell the fire. Imagine your own house burning.

FEBRUARY   The house is under renovation — deep fissures, cracks, walls spew dust. Plaster hills shore up corners of the room. Each ashen surface is painted with dabs of deep peach, or pomegranate, or plum. No one at home; only the guides asleep in narrow beds greet you on entering, surprised. In this house where a murder is unearthed, everything is in particles, snowing. Two women dotted in fragments wait behind an opaque partition. Arms entwined, they sway in the darkened room. Nothing interrupts their attentive gestures, yearnings spoken in the tender honey-tongued voices of lovers. Whispers discreet as the furred wings of moths, delicate as snow. Snow covers their hair like the years. Caught within this molecular space, a third woman is bludgeoned. It happens so quickly the other women don't move or cry out. This third woman appears frozen. Behind a screen, obscured from sight, the lovers wait in paralytic silence. The murderer, anonymous and undistinguished, produces a chisel to carve out the dead woman's hands; her fingers, lacquered scales of falling ice.

OCTOBER   Two women filmmakers address the audience. "If I had been a natural cook, I never would have been sucked into the cinema," says one. "If I had enjoyed vacuuming the house, I wouldn't have made this film," the other replies, leaning over to comfort a squalling baby.

The film begins: a sci-fi, set in Rio. Indigo ocean waves crash from the top of the screen to the bottom where a sea wall cuts the sinuous lines of surf. Without a moment's warning the wind rises. The space between water and stone slides open. Random objects — paper cups and lawn chairs, umbrellas and billboards — are swept into the black hole. Swivelling in their seats, the audience turns to view the projector's slit. Eyes shielded, looks shift along the dusty shaft of light. A fan blows cool cool air through the theatre.

JULY   "Destroy the form by which I please too well."

There. The trouble with love. The perfect feminist man, analogue to Zena's "entrepreneurial polyglot": more or less brilliant, more or less sexy, more or less politically correct. More or less perfectly charming. Understanding of distance and longing, he calls you on the phone. "Hello, hello." You tape his monologue on your answering machine and it plays back evenings. (After long years of talk, of taming the urgency to move, of travel to seaside locales.) Just calling to say hello.

Hello.

And to tell you . . . bye bye.

On a sailing trip to the Aegean, we float past blue onion rooftops leafed on a sunset surface. I am adamant about his presence; he is distracted, persistent, reminding me of his preference for mental travel. Our forbidden sleep on the island of Delos locates Apollo in place. The moonlit hours listen to underground waterways which still course below crumbled stairwell, sounding kitchen and temple. He shouts through a symmetrical opening in the ground; this dark echo calls him home.

DECEMBER   When no one is looking, reach through the broken glass of the bakery display. The pastries are doubly divine. Delicate puffed cylinders the size of fingers ooze *crème anglaise* tinted pink. You are not alone in sybaritic delight. A pastry slips from a neighbouring hand, splatters your boots. I am unable to resist. Without once catching bare wrist on jagged gap, I consume unwisely, but well. . . .

JANUARY   "The thoughts derived from this envy still continued to fill her mind."

Marvel at how the following improbable anatomical feat penetrates the issue. In front of the clinic, the signs address you: ABORTION IS A GREATER SIN THAN RAPE! Men and women gather, speak in loud voices, brandish pictures framed by the sky — photographs of bloody messes in tin cans. Young women, eyes averted, hasten by. To taunts of "baby killer," these women cry, "You have an unacknowledged hostility toward women."

"Fuck yourself," says an angry man from the crowd.

Precisely.

NOVEMBER   The story wouldn't stop writing she couldn't stop skirting the reductive, the biological.

MAY   Possibly I dream over and over of losing shoes so she will come possibly slide tongue along the long route back know it is a matter of time before fingers clicking lips the teeth "am I hurting?" drive up my wall sting the sounds hollow at neck urgent like furred female animals rifling eyes the crushed lips/cheeks/ teeth bared as in pain she is wet she is smelling wet shaking wet brow rain on her hair this yellow couched between my legs lose sight throat thin walls taste this aversion this body we bathe to forget white light instructs the room rearranges the furniture returns me to father framed in the doorway know that I am twelve know that he has taken his shorts his cock cradled in hand now offers this look the cool August evenings at sea full blown steamed edges gape dehiscent strain forms like sublimating slake out burst taut skin the lick the sing the lap of equilibrium

FEBRUARY 1920   "I broke off the treatment and advised her parents that if they set store by the therapeutic procedure it should be continued by a woman doctor."

APRIL   You crochet, finish the sleeves of the sweater in a luminescent silver. A pocket on the left breast bears a slit and a button where your nipple shows through. I mention this in case you haven't noticed. You dismiss my concern, dip your ample taffeta skirt in the breeze. It twirls languorously toward the centre of the room.

Nature made ferns for pure leaves
(a popular romance)

The reproduction of ferns by spores differs from that of seed-flowering plants in that it interposes a half step between each two generations. The single spore, a very minute body, germinates in dampness and shade, producing a little flat leaf-like body called the prothallium. On the underside of this the sex organs develop and fertilization occurs. . . . Then, after a long period, varying usually from 2 to 6 months, the first young fronds of the true fern appear.

E.L.D. Seymour

adders tongue   fern   beech   fern   bladder   fern   boulder   fern   brittle   fern

On her wedding night, the bride pricked needles in the backs of their hands. It was o.k.; she was a nurse. Near naked on the edge of the bed, the three joke about the holy trinity and the sanctity of their vows "to have and to hold." The younger woman, a mature nineteen, has wrapped herself in a couturier gown, a London gift from her Texas oilman: loden green tapestry circles her neck in tiny pearl buttons.

California fern chain fern Christmas fern cinnamon fern cloak

When the couple travels to Chicago for his film opening a week before their marriage, she visits their house daily to tend the groom-to-be's hardy border fern collection. In the mornings, the palms of her hands brush across fronds rolled tightly around their tips. Cautiously, she drowns a *pinna* or *pinnule*. Delicate mists pool at the bottom of a dozen terrariums: hand-like gestures of stag-horn ferns signal warnings from above the windows. Later in the week, in a panic, she retreats to his library's horticultural remedies for what she identifies as "blister-rust fungi." Lost forever is his fragile maidenhair, "the filmy lace-like fronds" now withered in ragged brown edges, unresponsive to her emergency bordeaux mixture. With no cure for his lady fern, a "rank grower" is suffocated by black mould scales.

Tonight she is their willing wedding present. After cocaine blasts a liquid passageway through their bodies, they suck each other. First, her tongue lips belly, then breasts; his mouth inhales dozens of lips like oysters. The bride waits her turn. His prick is small but hard and when entered she bites sharply skin (hers) is crawling
into the nipples of the bride who begins to cry. This sound substitutes for their breathing; the bride's wail this side of agony.
he sucked her lips, all of them. His prick was small but hard and when he entered she bit sharply into the bride's left nipple. Her wedding breasts heave with a cry which the young woman in green recognizes mid-orgasm: all the sound entails. Tailing the tale back home.

male fern   marginal shield fern   marsh fern   oak fern   mountain holly

After a while they rouse themselves and sit up, imagining they will talk to each other. The bride cautiously shakes out the bubbles of air, taps the needle with what appears to the others as teeth-clenched impatience. Needles reinsert through loose flesh behind the other palms: heroin fixed to calm jangled nerves. The plunging whoosh of breath intake too fast heady drift then loss of gasp   the exhalation wick burns like licks from tight electric guitars slicked under arteries. The dark behind pink lids something like sudden death. She is certain it can't go on and on like this until morning. They said there would be a punishment: electro-shock or brain damage or simple natural thunderbolt flames flung through patio doors. But even as she awaits her just desserts, the blender whirrs up special nourishing fruit drinks in preparation for impend-ing . . .

ostrich fern plypody fern rattlesnake fern royal fern sensitive fern

In the middle of her graduate school years, the groom revisits the city. In the evening, the young woman, less young, visits his hotel room. They glimpse themselves in a mirror framed in plaster flowers. After this glance, they will never look directly at each other. She sits on the edge of her chair and listens to him, eyes averted, talking talking about his pain as though words will cure him the way they had not cured her. After his soliloquy, she gives him her favourite poems about a gloomy double suicide: a hollow retort, a "manic ride into the bay." He talks about American violence; across the border, his handgun will be cradled in his palm.

shield   fern   silvery   fern   spleenwort   walking   fern   woodsia   fern

The future will open certain death to the groom. The van is parked close to the concrete railing's edge, carefully, on the L.A. freeway. . . . *his wife expects the younger woman who breezes her car, fast and open, along the Pacific edge of the continent.*.. Inside, the man harnessed bolt upright behind the wheel navigates his midnight corridor. His mid-life bride waits for him in a jacuzzi's air thick with damp ferns. . . . *refusing to mourn, holed up behind Malibu Beach Motel blinds, she calls from a pay phone a quarter mile down the road. Moments later at the door, roused from her bath, his wife says with silence her boy's away at school* . . . His eyes will be dead; a needle hangs suspended from the back of his hand. A blond son will be tucked into bed asleep beneath a picture of his favourite movie star, James Dean, for nostalgia's sake. . . . *she follows her up the stairs pulls back a rose-petal spread unwraps her robe skin lit round by the sea beginning with toes she will taste what she missed leaf arms through their longing* . . .

interrupted cinnamon lip deer mountain holly marsh silvery walking fern woodsia

Ramble on about this garden twenty years after the fact, memory's sweet task, watching a fresh snowfall, for nostalgia's sake. A green swath of skirt lifts high around permanent curls. Her breath words delicate as moonlit fronds. The silvering touches her with more than suburban biplay. Nothing transcendental. Nothing that doesn't require their tender flesh nicked with terrible closeness. Her hands hers form pointless claws tsk tsk how the shaded arch catches the nape of her neck again and again as though there might be an entrance here too.

"Tell me the truth about *Gado-Gado*"

for b

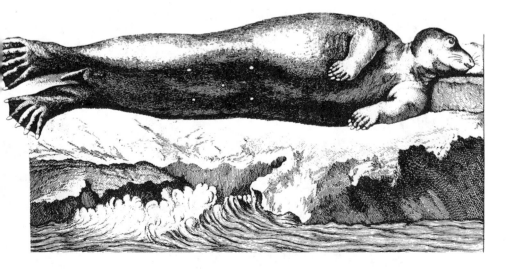

I ask as though you will know the answer. Up to your elbows in peanut butter and onion, you say nothing, knowing as I do the necessity of your silence. Oblivious, licking the bowl clean, the dog at our feet laughs.

1 CUP GOOD, PURE PEANUT BUTTER

We cook only what we can.

1/4 TSP. CAYENNE PEPPER (MORE TO TASTE)

At the sink, the water dances to your wrists, liking the difference.

1 TBS. HONEY

All apples, bananas and good fibre foods stand up and salute your arrival.

1-2 TSP. FRESHLY GRATED GINGER ROOT

You feed me more than I need, more than I would ever ask for, more than I want to admit wanting.

JUICE OF 1 LEMON

Add a pinch. Please.

2 MEDIUM CLOVES CRUSHED GARLIC

Across the table from the redheaded young woman, you remove my left cowboy boot, my sock with little animals running towards the toes. "Do you like the redhead?" I ask in silence. "Do you?" you reply, nervously. Lifting up my bare foot, you lick me dry. No one notices the redhead blinking herself to speak brilliantly.

1 BAY LEAF

A crash of something at breakfast flies through the window. Breathless glass everywhere. You look up from your Wheaties, scared. Me too. A sign of sacrifice links our morning rites to feathered sound. A chicken dead at our feet.

DASH OF TAMARI

Since you've been gone, the dog looks at me with one eye. The other turns inward.

1/2-1 TSP. SALT

Alone, I open the box, snip off the plastic corner, bake for twenty-five minutes, empty out the contents from the tin-foil tray, eat while reading again. It is quiet enough.

1 TBS. CIDER VINEGAR

Grandmother plucked up the ducks every summer when she visited the east, as though this were the prairies and there was still laughter among the hired hands at dinner. As though there had been laughter at dinner among the hungry mouths itching for more. As though the hungry mouths could speak now to this fêted family. To the tune of the dishwasher moaning overstuffed, my grandma remembers to count the ways.

3 CUPS WATER

At fourteen, she washed her hair and thought about men and cleanliness. The song about washing them out. Crying now, the soapy water fills with her tears; she musters up the courage to tell her father "I love you . . ." in spite of . . . (she doesn't know). At the kitchen table, her father weeps on hearing her words' longing for his. He recognizes something she doesn't know; she cries too.

1 CUP CHOPPED ONION

The eggs at breakfast make lumps in our bodies we cannot see. Usually, they don't bother us, just show up like little x's on some sound screen of new technology. The nurse shows how the little eggs at breakfast look just like this x. Their hooked ends catch onto passing organs, make their own musical dirge in the dark.

PIECES OF EGG

Pressed up against a beige refrigerator, she says she has a toothache, just like the little girl in *The Lesson* pushing, pushing for recognition. As though I had something to add, I tell her "yes," she has a toothache. Then she dies. Her jaw rotting from something she ate or didn't. Something she said or wouldn't. Or her jaw rotting inside out of her just like that.

TOASTED SEEDS AND NUTS

Nibbling on hors d'oeuvres, they talk about love, work, death and marriage. She had performed the latter; he had not. That made all the difference. Squishing the inky sea of roe through his teeth in response, he told his own stories which are his and which she can't repeat.

Why marry? Why make the familiar strange? she thought, saying aloud, "The problem with weddings is in the cakes." What the icing shores up lies hidden in empty centres. This insight hadn't surfaced until she read cautionary advice about the "anti-social family" and boycotted all things wedding. Yes yes, she admitted, she had passionately kissed the groom's sister in the washroom at the engagement party, an out-of-wedlock scandal. To memorialize the occasion, she collected tiers of brightly coloured Italian plum tomato cans arranged in a pyramid of pleasuring women's smiles, rosy breasts and hands dripping *pomidoro pelati*.

What about him?

His pessimism surprised even himself. He announced he wanted to marry so later, on separating, divorce would grant them the sense of an ending. This irrationality seemed to her perfectly sensible since she had married the first and only time when she was certain of her imminent death. Just in case, she wanted someone to mourn her loss at the funeral. Someone official like a husband with a loop of gold glint round the finger that had obviously loved her. Her fearful desire had been understandable considering the circumstances, but she doubted whether it was a good enough excuse for a marriage she never wanted to speak of or repeat.

"Could we have years of pre-nuptial parties instead?"

A DRIZZLE OF SESAME OIL

At a gathering of island people, cod tongues burst on our tongues. Tender pockets of ocean water drown our throats' speeches. I pass the test. Your old neighbour writes home to her sister about this dinner. It seems unwittingly I passed *this* test and the one about bakeapple jam seeds stuck between incisors. But will I survive the skill testing which serves up fog, roadside moose meat or the roar of lions at sea?

Lucrece

We resolve to invent passion   imagine it as beyond
the circling of tongues   As the cold rage
which changes something
                    Claire Harris

Do not stand at my grave and weep,
I am not there. I do not sleep. . . .
Do not stand at my grave and cry,
I am not there. I did not die.

The suicidal omen began in classical Rome where Lucrece was proclaimed the most virtuous wife in a city-wide competition. Instead of revelling like the other wives in their husbands' absence, Lucrece had faithfully remained at home spinning. Although an unofficial winner of the contest, her husband Collatinus puffed up with pride on the battlefield where his tent was pitched. A few days after the competition, Lucrece was visited by the son of Sextus Tarquinius, the ruling tyrant, who vowed to "test" her virtue. At midnight, as part of his examination, Sextus crept in to the sleeping Lucrece and raped her while she dreamed. The next morning, all Rome percolated with rumours of this violation. Friends, husband and family gathered to console Lucrece, assuring her, "You submitted to a tyrant's lust only when he threatened he was going to cut your throat, murder a servant, and place him nude beside your body."

With a quick thrust of the knife, she demonstrated what she had always been taught about the necessity of virtue. To avenge her suicide, her husband's friend Brutus cried out "freedom" over Lucrece's unchaste body. The ruling tyrants, vanquished in the din of Brutus's growing fame, drowned out the long wailing night of Lucrece.

Episodic Memory

*Very singular is the art of this invisible art of memory . . .
concentrating its choice on irregular places and avoiding
symmetrical orders.*
Frances Yates

1. March 29, 1989, at 2:30 a.m. in a half dream state she heard the whining of

truck tires itching for traction and creak crash of wood. Silence for a moment, the sound of a truck shifting gears and position, more tire whines and wood wail. She awoke knowing the sounds were real: someone had demolished her backyard fence. Awake for hours, she talked herself out of what she imagined as paranoid fantasy. Cold morning light and her fence has disappeared.

2. Before the cop arrived, Lucrece had asked her journal:

"In a reactionary province, how does the Law read my story?"

3. "Yup. Sure is vandalism. Ropes and a truck and look at these boot prints. Male.

Public mischief. Lady, d'ya have any enemies?
   I have no personal life. How can I have enemies?
   What kinda work d'ya do? .
   I'm a teacher.
   Whad'ya teach?
   Writing.
   Whad'ya been teaching?
   Lesbian love poems.
   Thaddle do it.
   That's it?
   Yep.
   (Silent weeping.)
   No. Don't start that now, little lady. No use cryin about it. If I was you I'd just whip up another one of them creative lectures, git my fence back up, and flush em out. Call 911 and we'll be here in a flash. Ya gotta act like a bear. Bears looks real gentle from far off, but get up close and the bear gives ya a swipe and yur dead. Or a rattlesnake — looks quiet in the hot noonday sun. Me, I'm a hunter; they call me the Mad Trapper. Got some of them conibear traps up on the farm. Illegal ya know. If I wuz you, I'd get one of them traps and put them in my backyard. Yep. Public mischief alright. No suspects.

(In recounting this story, Lucrece is almost reassured. She has the numbers to prove it — file number 89-45300 investigated by badge number 638. The interview takes place in his official car and ends when he rummages in his papers to find his card, a hotline number for anxiety counselling as though, he says, she had been raped.

4. "I've been thinking since I returned home about the memo I sent to you. The

tearing down of the fence is a convincing narrative for listeners like the police, but is it a good story? My fence is not a linguistic construct; when it ripped apart, the wood moaned and crashed. The wreckage is no mere vulgar displacement: the frat boys did not mistake my house for the domicile of outraged private property preservers. Neither do I imagine that local developers descended to retaliate for my public civic activism, since my criticism was more theoretical than inciting. Nor is it probable that a Muslim fundamentalist retaliated against my support for Salmon Rushdie. Had there been any local violence, surely balconies would have been ripped off, a gesture blessed with the verticality of transcendence. No, this is the job of urban cowboys: fundamentalists whose city fences belie cattle rustlers and north country homesteads."

5. This wasn't a story. The story was not a story. The fence was down, shattered. The

dean, the chair, the colleagues, the corridor-mates, the neighbours, the students had been notified. Every telling apparently increased her anxiety until finally the entire room heard her break down.

6. The speaking paralysis revealed only this. Lucrece stayed in bed and did not move

in spite of her assured knowledge. She had heard the ice whine under the tires. She stayed in bed. She did nothing. Had she remembered other midnight violations?

7. What stands in for intelligence?

photographic memory?
workaholism?
instant recall?

Semantic Memory

I do not imagine anyone could be excused from
finding a solution to this mystery.
Nicole Brossard

1. "If I weren't in love I wouldn't be here.

I wouldn't be — without expressing my love for you."
Misery makes her more cultured.

2. The man who had a heart noted he had probably been the one

to sacrifice "the relationship." He said he must not have wanted her; he planned it that way, the way she left as a result of his pressure for greater "intimacy." She fell into the trap knowing it was no trap. It didn't matter. This was the way it was as though she could choose not choose her next move.

3. In her draft of adult life, the preface examines "regret."

Listen for weeping in the verb *to greet.*
    What did Lucrece know about living that was not loss? His note to her began *my love.* Later, *my love* reappeared in every conversation hinged to the intimate pivot *tu.* So easy to hear to not hear the lawn chairs billow inside out this August storm. Lucrece remembered their bodies together; *ing* words appropriate for her longing. What was it that made her so eager to write the ending? Her arms reached out to embrace and then, muscles tensed, pushed him away. When he began to press her to give up the work she loved, she felt threatened to something like the core of her being. Her being? Her legs were filigreed veins; she would be dead lace in another few decades.

4. Sick of urban spill, Lucrece heads west along the Yellowhead.

Everywhere in Saskatchewan, signs of life stick up like thumbs or something less appealing. She works to develop character here: the car, the fit of the glove along the smooth hollowed surface of the wheel; the car, the hat tipped wildly back to permed curls; the car, Joan Didion's darling. (If this is Tuesday, take the highway!)

5. OK Tuesday or Friday. Bison along the roadside. Sky:

brilliant blue lanced with sunlight pours dangerously towards pupils the opposite of dilation pin pointed now in her head faced west. Due.

6. OK in the car facing west between her right ear lobe and temple,

a slit opens up the middle of the night, slide of a man framed in white cardboard just like a dream, the man stands in front of a basinette or changing table, the whiteness of the plastic quilted to embroidered shadow. He is touching the baby somewhere, her genitals, and now that she has read *Don't*, the story of incest with numbered paragraphs, she wonders for a moment whether this memory is no more than a crossover from that elsewhere.

7. OK in the car facing west the projector of her brain, her

mind's eye refocuses, tears vaseline the lens. Like this she says: OK in the car facing west there is a slide. The prospector, the daddy, or maybe any old uncle man. The dark-haired man.

8. OK in the car facing west Lucrece calls momma

momma. Did this happen? No dear. We would never have left you with the men. They wouldn't know what to do with you. We wouldn't not do our job, abandon you to others. In this last sentence no note of speculation tempers momma's voice.

9. Storymaking, the inside outside story

the inside story a sordid affair: the outside story business as usual: between the two, nothing more than two dots dark eyes stare out of baby head: two tiny memories of somewhere else someone else: the body remembers the tender skin pulled inside the thickened pressure of fingertips knuckle deep now and again the thrust is that the word or is it play stranger play daddy play uncle or big bad wolf: the tender slip of a thing legs buck fat broncos: see see said the blind man: she looked again radiant in waves

10. After Lucrece's dream, her body's pain

shifts ground from her vague anxious doubts to various corridors; her vagina aches without reason and all day long she smells shit as though a dog were in every corner, or under the stairs. She smells it everywhere on her skin. This mixture of mental debris and lived surfaces.

11. Lucrece pretends the story is one thing then another,

imagines herself inside a new ending. It follows. Years later the structure repeats itself. Clinging to vision, she dressed up like Margaret Atwood in Spanish. Story. Story. Her heartbeat takes these bare bones and tells this:

Don't start again.

12. In this paragraph, she cannot take root inside words.

This side of the familiar is spoken in a conversation she wasn't supposed to hear when she was twelve, an event she never told. Her mother said, "The others are too little." The daughter, not quite her, but not quite separate, "Daddy's girl," would stay behind. In the living room, she listened to "Daddy," so scary, so full of life he melted ivory with Brazilian tunes, songs about dancing sidewalks and limbs, tanned beached breasts, songs about apples — music like violins like horror movies which make her squirm too close to come, paralysed in her seat. Or the broken mirror on the bathroom door accomplished Sunday mornings in hide and seek after she left church, knowing her way to hell and jesus in the mailbox at the end of the drive called "starling," eye-glint nest, thick straw.

13. In the cedar V of the mountains, she narrates her story

to the strict editorial guidelines of Harlequin Industries. Floating through a hotel window, she hopes to recognize "the facts" in her dream's telling clues which surface after thirty-seven years. "But which hotel?" she muses fitfully. Was it The Hume, now renamed The Heritage Hotel, with a long encrusted history of stained glass and buried balustrades? Or was her sense of connection to these ten-foot fireplaces no more than an inflation of her modest class origins? Did she remember her childhood self in The Old Nelson, formerly The New Grand, whose painted-over deco signs had looked across the harbour before three-storey buildings interrupted the view? Or was her child self at play behind the reception desk now hidden behind sliding doors in The Royal Hotel? Drunks in The Royal's saloon mimic the sombre, bearded men photographed on the wall; slumped across tables, their half-closed eyes mine wood-sidewalk stories of too long ago.

Later on the telephone, her mother confirms they had all lived in The Royal. Lucrece laughs nervously, "But The Royal's a dive."

"Yes, it always was," confessed Momma, "but the miners were nice and looked after you."

Dive deep down into this "looked after." No blame.

Thick fists pound at the door as memory crashes into the middle of the hotel room. Drunk, the dark-haired miner stumbles forward to snatch Lucrece from her grandmother's arms.

Nanna explains, "The prospectors liked you and always gave you gold nuggets."

"We wouldn't leave you with the men. They wouldn't have known what to do with you."

14. The first time she makes love, her body will split apart, her

skin flushes with pleasure, while inside a sharp gasp heaves all her air into the living room. Her body, kissed into sudden death, stops breathing. At her side, a frightened boy struggles to make her speak but she wouldn't, couldn't open her eyes to tell him. She wasn't angry, she told herself, just acting stupid about all this breathing she had read about how you do it the first time and then, like swimming, again. Just breathe, she told herself, her not listening body naked beneath her, afloat in his panicked arms. The clatter of the back door, his fearful path to the car, red top down, blue roof, chill air between her and the vinyl seat. A cold flesh shock and her mouth sputters to life just in time, she thinks, to avoid public knowledge and certain humiliation. This must be love.

When she remembers to tell her story in the middle of a different love, she is told, "Sometimes, the first time, girls can't breathe. Their tongues remember their mouths filled up."

Local Memory

*The Second Captain or the Circular Line is a man in a circle with legs and arms
extended. On the places of this man's body we are to remember the four elements and
the eleven heavens: earth, feet; water, knee; air, flank; fire, arm; Luna, right hand;
Mercury, fore-arm; Venus, shoulder; Sol, head; Mars, left shoulder; Jupiter, left
fore-arm; Saturn, left hand; sphere of fixed stars, left shoulder; christalline sphere,
waist; primum mobile, knees; Paradise, under left foot.*

"The Art of Local Memory"
Agostino de Riccio (1595)

1. Hands

A knife is only a knife; a dagger, a dagger. Dissolve memory of past violations
at the hand of White doctor, professor, male man of the street. You, Doctor,
raped me in the cool afternoon sliced thin in the shade of venetian blinds. This
afternoon, white sheets wrap round my mind; yours masked behind a bearded
lip. Lift up my sleep. My body slides towards you. Your fingers smooth the
sheets, adjust the stirrups. You tell me you love me as though when I am no
longer fifteen, I might repeat this medical history. Hands stroke soft across my
belly, my nipples. (Do you have the answers to my questions? Was my arm held
out for a moment too long? Did my shy gaze seduce?) I watch you rape me
somewhere below these legs the edge of the table, a white paper smock. My
words kick at your thighs, moving and oblivious to everything but silence —
your accomplice in this examination for discovery.

2. Hands

On another continent, whirling through the marketplace, the seaside cafe, the
grand marble lobby of your hotel, I am "sister" in your alphabet — the waiter
is your uncle and later the family circle widens to hold your widower's tale. In
the disco we dance. Mute women veiled in turquoise lounge with large men
who smile at my orange juice, fresh and sweet.
   You try to rape me on the Moroccan coast beside the moon you want me to
love. A movie projector would have been less mechanically minded. You pull
me towards you, pretend your desire is mine. How could I not be lured to the
water's edge of farewell promises, the desert moon at our feet? Your muffled
sounds of pleasure will be a prelude to my paralytic retreat. I am nineteen and
I can scream on the beach to no one in particular but the burnous-hooded man
who arrives, you say, "a thief." Later you tell me he was a policeman. What

possessed me to believe you had my best interests at heart? When I jump out of the car like a stupid Hollywood heroine, my ankle cracking in the night, you follow in your car, anticipate my death at the hands of drunken strangers.

3. Hands

This time you knock on the door, call me "friend," visit late in the evening after the bar to show me your photographs. Behind the balcony of this Dakar hotel, the hot yellow of the prairie field is bleached a less violent shade, the colour of your lost French lover's hair. You show me the photograph of your Catherine Deneuve look-alike, a delicate shadow on her neck. Was this the hollow heart of her collar-bone or a sign imprinted by her blue knowledge of you? Through thick tropical air, you reach towards me; my arms hold out in dramatic jest and laugh until your powerful hand slaps my face, my body wrung out to the floor. I cry and cry out and you tell me, what do I expect? as though I knew how naïve I could be in order to plan not plan this occasion when you rape me. I cry out through this long night, voices in the hall so close I make out drunken love whispers. In the morning, I will get up from the bed. In the morning I would rise, rise up from the bed. Would rise over and over in my mind, wash my face, my hands once more in a shallow sink. Wait for any sun to light up this unknown city to shelter me from you, the stench of your companionable disguise. (From beside me on the bed, his eyes look at me with something like affection. He remembers the ship's deck — how we laughed at the dark oceans between us, the long passage by sea where we met in the unsteady rhythm around Gibraltar, the sounds of Lanzerote's black lava cave. Tonight, white sands from Agadir's maze sift from our hair as I fall passive to the floor.

In the confused paralysis of these moments, I become wise about possible endings. You pull me towards you; my voice careens through your seashell ear. Enraged, you stop or look without seeing or simply watch as you move towards me again and again and again. This is fear, or first-world envy, or a domestic race war detached from my being. I would stop writing this story if there were any other ending than my zero of nothing turned liquid sound. Unbound, inside the blank middle of pain, my flesh leaks across the room under a wooden door towards a light. Shutters slash pain through this body this steaming Dakar hotel room called, I can't remember, down the beach from moonlit dance bars called, I can't remember, down the road from Isle St. Louis where no white man was ever imprisoned for violating your sisters.

I won't name this occasion rape for fifteen years.

4. Hands

I can't remember.

Tiny feet kick out the rage of a baby girl's white quilt. She dreams lions and tigers escape through cracks in the wood floor. The white lace of her blanket catches in the futile directions of a top-hatted animal tamer who dies like all the others. Momma. Daddy.

In the waking dream, a dark-haired faceless man (a babysitter? a prospector?) is outlined in the window. His hands strangely turned and moving. Her infant legs flail out against the mystery.

5. Paradise, under left foot

Tonight across the roses in this new garden, I call you rapist one by one. Would my questions stir you now from your Albertan or African sun? I wait while you circle over Paris. I wait for you in Moscow. In Montreal, I see you in the street. In London, I wait for your return home. In Washington, in Peking, I wait for your stories of lapses in decorum or ideological privilege. I wait for you in your father's house. I am at home in the world. In cities, my mouth opens to corridors, cries through stairwells and broken bars, smashes locked doors, the shield of a man asleep in the still quiet returned to our bed. My unquiet breast beats inside the rhythms of your pulsed body. Beats unbeaten in your ear.

Lucrece Writes

Writing is a compensation for life, not a substitute, for Lucrece lives full of rich lively pleasures. Writing stands in for nostalgia, takes the place of recovery. Memory on the move in writing stands aside takes up alphabet postures as though there were a place for "you."

Hands: regret runs the length of this column ridged a circumference her hands cannot reach round.

Hands: at three o'clock, memory sifts restless; "a writing in black and white, using shadow and light."

Hands: her twelve-year-old girl hand strikes a match to scorch edges of nothing, her first written words, *oh god oh god oh god*

Hands: texture slash of ribbons remind this pebbled concrete.

Hands: lined like small leaves wrenched from aspen in May.

Hands: summer delphiniums purple in the wind while I imagine the past tense of poison pressed between my ribs.

Hands: "let loose your knotted fever, your cancer around my heart."

Lucrece

In the main gallery, the painting of Lucrece leaps from the wall. Her words are etched in blood: *What woman will be safe if Lucrece has been raped? My appropriate desire of chastity did me an injury. The abominable adulterer wanted to assault not my beauty but my chastity. Can I endure anymore in this corrupted body? Pour forth this blood as an omen.*

Green on this gallery's easel, frame now removed, this canvas restores Lucrece to herself. A female actor in history's tragic drama, Lucrece teaches us to read and write ourselves. Her memory, preserved in the domed tip of her headdress, resists the frame's chaste borders. Transparent filigreed ribbons tease out the artist's unpainted margin. This veil of lace gathers into questions: How many centuries passed before someone unmasked the pale edges of her body's story? How did Lucrece's "amnesia of the unconscious" make her suicide inevitable? What thoughts passed through the artist's mind, hiding her traces with gilt? To how many women did the verdant drapery of her sleeve refuse to speak? How much of Lucrece is left to my imagination?

Every day for the past week I've returned to this conversation I imagine with Lucrece. Together we rewrite possible endings. To tell her tale, we are obliged to reveal that this original Lucrece was no heroine; her motives remain compromised in the unexamined privilege of her proclamation, "Unless I kill myself, never will you trust that I preferred to escape infamy than death. Who will ever believe that he terrified me with the killing of the slave and that I feared more the possible disgrace of a slave joined to me than death, unless, by the strength and courage of dying, I will prove it?" No heroine to speak of. Our long women's memory teaches us pleasures beyond *carpe diem*, the cry which never asks whose days are worth seizing.

In the bustle of the Belgian gallery, the painting's surfaces refuse to bind Lucrece. Pale tissue slides open to receive the dagger's sharp edge, her feint driven home. Along her belly, drops of lifeblood slide vertical; an open palm hides their dark journey. Her suicide exceeds this portrait's understanding. Why do her breasts, perfectly round, emerge from behind the gauze blouse to please . . . ? The artist? Only her mouth begins to speak in lines set hard with betrayal. Scarlet-rimmed eyes question the rage. Her lips open to the breath of pain grasped.

Song of Lucrece

The boundaries of Lucrece's history are detailed in the pergola's aslant determination. In this obscure light, I write her lace bodice unbuttoned each morning in verbs, invincible. Across this new ending, the amorous arouses exclamatory. Lucrece's bloody veil unstops bliss, sets sail along her belly, this side of lunar reflection. Flesh mends flesh, minds her body's scarred signature . . .

"I did not die."

Acknowledgements

My thanks to the editors of the following publications where versions of some of this writing have been published: *The American Voice, Best Canadian Essays 1990, Border/lines, Contemporary Verse 2, How(ever), Impulse, Rampike, Taking Our Time: Feminist Perspectives on Temporality, Tessera.* "excerpts from the journals of Alberta Borges" was first published as a Greensleeve Publishing Chapbook.

I wish to acknowledge support from West Word I, Gillian Smith's Womanspace, The Banff Centre's Leighton Artist Colony and the Ontario Arts Council. I am grateful for the expertise of David Arnason, Marilyn Morton and Paula Kelly at Turnstone Press. Angela Julian Day and Isabel Huggan were early conspirators. My thanks to Di Brandt, Daphne Marlatt, Gail Scott, Betsy Warland and Sandra Birdsell. Pam Banting, Pauline Butling, Mary Howes, Neil Scotten, Gerry Hill and Fred Wah gathered in stirring writerly talk for a good year. Debbie Gorham, Christine Davis, Pat Elliot, Kim Echlin, Ben Jones, William Lane, Susan Shirriff and Jane Springer understood the telltale signs. Jay MacPherson taught me Persephone's rhythms. Eli Mandel, Claudine Potvin and Brian Rusted encouraged me to leap the institutional ditch between scholar and writer. My mother and Aunt Peg gave in to my resistance, having cultivated their own. Ward and Scott shared their stories. This book is dedicated to the memory of Robert Handforth (1949-1988), and to those rebellious women who work with the words to tell.

Notes

tell tale signs
Tony Cade Bambara. *Gorilla, My Love.* Random House, 1972; Maurice Blanchot. *Death Sentence.* Station Hill, 1976; Marguerite Duras. *The War: A Memoir.* Pantheon, 1986; Gustave Flaubert. *Emma Bovary.* 1857. Bantam, 1981; Jane Gallop. *Thinking Through the Body.* Columbia University Press, 1988; Peter Handke. *Offending the Audience, Kaspar and Other Plays.* Noonday Press, 1969; Lyn Hejinian. *My Life.* Sun & Moon Press, 1987; Arthur Jacobs. *A New Dictionary of Music.* Penguin, 1967; Daphne Marlatt. *Our Lives.* Oolichan Books, 1980; The Toronto Parkdale community newspaper; Suniti Namjoshi and Gillian Hanscombe. *Paper and Flesh.* Ragweed Press, 1986; Fred Wah. *Music at the Heart of Thinking.* Red Deer College Press, 1987.

A Family Holiday in Sunny Puerto Plata
Jessica Benjamin. *The Bonds of Love: Psychoanalysis, Feminism, and the Problem of Domination.* Pantheon, 1988; Selden Rodman. *Quisqueya: A History of the Dominican Republic.* University of Washington Press, 1964.

Of women and fish
Beverley Dahlen. *A Reading (11-17).* Potes & Poets, 1989; Anne Sexton. *The Collected Poems of Anne Sexton.* Houghton Mifflin, 1981; Phyllis Webb. *Wilson's Bowl.* Coach House Press, 1980.

on the couch and Fundamental Rule
Mary Butts. *Imaginary Letters.* 1928. Talonbooks, 1979; H.D. *Tribute to Freud.* New Directions, 1956; Ovid. *Metamorphosis.* Penguin, 1955; *The Globe & Mail.*

Nature made ferns for pure leaves
E.L.D. Seymour, ed. *The Illustrated Home Garden Guide.* J.J. Little & Ives, 1961. The title is from Henry David Thoreau.

"Tell me the truth about *Gado-Gado*"
Gado-Gado, "an Indonesian dish with spicy peanut sauce," is prepared according to this recipe in *The Moosewood Cookbook.* Compiled, edited, illustrated and hand-lettered by Mollie Katzen. Ten Speed Press, 1977: 104.

Lucrece

Quotations are from Coluccio Salutati's *Declamatio Lucretiae*, a thirteenth-century Florentine retelling of Lucrece's story. The manuscript's translation is by Stephanie H. Jed in her study, *Chaste Thinking: The Rape of Lucretia and the Birth of Humanism* (Indiana University Press, 1989).

The visual images in this book are from the following sources. The author wishes to thank the artists and publishers for permission to reproduce copyrighted images.

Front cover photo: detail from *Gabrielle d'Estrées et une de ses soeurs*. Artist unknown. Reprinted by permission of the Musée du Louvre, Paris.

Pages 11, 16, 27, 34, 38, 39, 40, 41, 42, 43: from William Rowe, *Machinery and Mechanical Devices: A Treasury of Nineteenth-Century Cuts* (New York: Dover, 1987). Reprinted by permission.

Pages 14, 15, 17, 18, 20, 21, 22, 23, 26, 28, 30, 31, 32, 35, 44, 45, 47, 49, 97, 109, 121 and 125: from J.G. Heck, *The Complete Encyclopedia of Illustration* (New York: Park Lane, 1979).

Pages 19 and 113: from Judy M. Johnson, *Spot Illustrations from Women's Magazines of the Teens and Twenties* (New York: Dover, 1989).

Page 24: from Gerd Gruneisl and Wolfgang Zacharias, eds., *PA-Schnippelbuch Nr. 1* (Munich: Padagogische Aktion e.V., 1981).

Page 25: from *Tavole Imbandite* (Milan: SugarCo Edizioni S.r.l., 1981).

Pages 29 and 33: from Jim Harter, *Men: A Pictorial Archive from Nineteenth-Century Sources* (New York: Dover, 1980).

Pages 36 and 37: from Leslie Cabarga, *Advertising Spot Illustrations of the Twenties and Thirties: 1,593 Cuts* (New York: Dover, 1989).

Pages 46, 48 and 51: from Frank Dean, *Will Rogers Rope Tricks* (Colorado Springs: Western Horseman Publishers, 1969). Reprinted by permission.

Page 50: from L. Cabarga, R. Greene and M. Cruz, *1,001 Advertising Cuts from the Twenties and Thirties* (New York: Dover, 1987).

Page 53: original drawing for "excerpts from the journals of Alberta Borges" by Sandra Meigs. First published in *excerpts from the journals of Alberta Borges* (Edmonton: Gleensleeve Publishing, 1991). Reprinted by permission.

Pages 99 and 133: from Janet Evans, *The Natural Science Picture Sourcebook* (New York: Van Nostrand Reinhold, 1984).

Page 137: detail: photographic transparency 7' x 5', from *Icon* (1990) by Barbara Steinman. Reprinted by permission.

Writer and editor Janice Williamson teaches English and Women's Studies at the University of Alberta, and has many scholarly publications and feminist writings to her credit, including *Up and Doing: Canadian Women and Peace* (with Deborah Gorham). She edited the forthcoming publication *Sounding the Difference: Conversations with Seventeen Canadian Women Writers*, and is at work on a cultural study of West Edmonton Mall and a book of innovative non-fiction.